GW00726682

The City of Light

The Secret of the Tirthas

Steve Griffin

For Anna

&

In Mem. Pamela Isobel Lilian Korn

Contents

Prologue

Twenty years. Twenty years his secret. *And now this...*

The old man closed his journal and peered out into the night. The moon hung low in the sky, illuminating the crisp foliage of the lawn and hedges. The metal face of the sundial shone with reflected light. Everything in his garden was peaceful, but still he felt anxious.

He was sure the intruder was using the tirtha to reach Kashi, the City of Light.

That morning, he had gone out early and again discovered footprints in the dew. As usual, they led to the statue of Shiva in the Indian garden, and stopped. Despite a painstaking search, he could find no footprints leading away from the statue. The intruder *must* have used the portal.

Now, leaning back in his chair, the old man wondered what to do. Should he set a trap, or try and get some kind of night-time camera? Or perhaps he should go to Kashi and speak to Bakir? For some time he'd been considering sharing the secret of the tirthas with the Hindu priest, his oldest friend. Not only would Bakir be fascinated by the portals, but he might also be able to help find out what the intruder was doing. Most importantly, he would understand the need to keep the tirthas secret.

Finally, the old man made his decision and stood up. He pulled a biscuit from his pocket and tossed it to the small, curly-haired dog lying in front of the fire. The dog caught it easily and began crunching.

'Come on, Mr Tubs,' he said, and the dog sprang to its feet. The old man stood the fireguard in front of the embers, then opened the glass-panelled door by his desk and stepped out into the night. Followed by the dog, he crossed the lawn towards a gap in the semi-circular hedge – and froze, as a twig snapped up ahead.

Someone was there.

He knew at once that it must be the intruder. *Who else would be in his garden late at night?*

Mr Tubs emitted a whine and the old man spun round at him, pressing a finger to his lips and *shushing*. He hurried to the gap and peered down the narrow, hedge-lined corridor beyond. He glimpsed a dark shape, disappearing into the garden at the end – *the Indian garden*.

The old man ran down the corridor and followed the intruder into the enclosure. The statue marking the portal – a large, bronze casting of Lord Shiva, dancing on the demon of ignorance and fear – was hidden behind a rhododendron bush that divided the garden in two. He rushed past the bush and saw the magnificent moonlit statue, surrounded by its circle of jagged bronze flame.

And there, standing on the lawn before it, was a dark, cloaked figure.

'You there!' the old man cried. 'Who are you?'

The intruder straightened, but did not turn around.

'Come on,' said the old man, striding forward. 'Enough of this. Show your face!'

The figure obliged, spinning round and flinging back the hood.

In his last moments of shock, despite the fatal explosion of blood vessels around his heart and the awful distortion of the face before him, the old man finally knew who the intruder was…

Chapter 1: Rowan Cottage

'That dog stinks.'

'He's been living on a farm for weeks.'

'You'll have to give him a bath as soon as we get there. The Bennetts obviously never bothered.'

Lizzie's scowl quickly vanished as the little dog perched on her lap tipped back his head and licked one of her eyebrows.

'Mr Tubs!' she said, squeezing him tighter.

'What a stupid name,' said her mum, glancing down at the dog as she drove. 'Typical of your great-uncle. Why couldn't he have called it something normal like... like... Rover?'

'Rover?' Lizzie looked out of the window and hid her smile. A gloomy tunnel of trees had replaced the grey, wintry fields of the Herefordshire countryside. Up ahead a side lane was signposted to a place called Hebley. Now her mum had pointed it out, Lizzie couldn't help notice the dog did have a slight farmyard *hum* about him.

'Where is it?' muttered her mum. 'We should have seen the sign by now.'

There was a crunch of gears as she took the car round a bend, and then Mr Tubs leaned forward and pressed his nose on the windscreen. He began to whine. A hand-painted sign for Rowan Cottage appeared up ahead.

'At last!' said Lizzie's mum, swinging the car sharply into the hedge-lined drive. Lizzie caught Mr Tubs as he lurched sideways.

Gravel crackled beneath the tyres of the old Volvo as her mum navigated the narrow drive and drew to a halt. She switched off the engine and all three stared at the building in front of them.

Rowan Cottage was a long, two-storey house with brown, unpainted timbers and grubby, pink-washed plaster. The thatched roof was overgrown with moss. Small windows punctured the deep walls. In the fading light of the late November afternoon, it looked cold, dark, and unlived in – which of course it was, having been empty since Lizzie's great-uncle had died of a heart attack. Lizzie felt a surge of misery and wondered whether she'd ever be able to think of such an old, dingy place as home.

Her mum sighed. 'Look at the state of it...'

Lizzie kept quiet as her mum fumbled in her handbag for the keys they'd collected earlier from the solicitor. Back in Croydon, Lizzie had done her best to persuade her mum not to uproot them again so soon. *She'd just started getting used to her new school, making some friends.* But her mum had, as usual, made *their* mind up.

'Come on,' said her mum, pulling the keys out of her bag. She climbed out of the car and crossed the drive to the cottage. She opened the front door and, after a few seconds standing and looking, disappeared inside.

'You *are* going to need a bath,' said Lizzie, as she reached round Mr Tubs and opened the car door. The dog leapt out and ran towards the house. He stopped briefly at the front door to look back at her, before turning and scurrying inside.

Lizzie smiled. *At least she had Mr Tubs.*

She followed the dog into the house, crossing the threshold into a musty, low-ceilinged hall with wooden beams and bare floorboards. In the gloomy afternoon light she saw the walls were covered with objects – not just pictures, but also sculptures and odd things such as rugs, swords, and puppets. Beside her face was a fierce African-looking mask of polished wood, with slanted eyeholes and gashes on the cheeks. She reached for the light to get a better look, but when she flicked the switch nothing happened.

'Mum – there's no lights.'

'Hold on – I think I've found the electricity,' said her mum, crouching down beneath the staircase.

After a few bumps, curses, and doggy whines, there was a loud clack and the light went on. Lizzie's eyes widened as her great-uncle's curios were brought to life. Amid more clutter than a small museum she spotted a map with oceans full of monsters, a black-and-white etching of a castle, a sharp-faced little puppet in a purple ceremonial outfit, and a plastercast of a man's head with ivy worming out through his mouth and nostrils.

'Yuck!' said her mum. 'I'd forgotten just how much junk he had.' She picked up her handbag from the floor and fumbled for her cigarettes.

'Where'd he get it all?' asked Lizzie.

'God knows. On his trips abroad, I suppose,' said her mum, squinting at a miniature painting of women dancing in chiffon dresses in a glade. She lit her cigarette.

'Dad would have loved this,' said Lizzie, reaching up and touching the African mask. Even as she said it, she felt her mum bristle.

'Yes, he would,' she said, breathing out a plume of smoke. 'And this,' she added curtly, looking at the small painting.

'Mum…' said Lizzie.

'What?'

'Don't be like that.'

'He was no saint, Lizzie,' said her mum, drawing again on her cigarette.

'What do you mean?'

'You know what I mean. We'd never have had to move here if it wasn't for him.'

'But we didn't *have* to move here.'

'We couldn't live in your gran's flat forever – it's too small. You know that as well as I do.'

'Yes, but…'

'And we'd never have had to live with her in the first place, if your father had kept his affairs in order, and taken out insurance like he said he had.' Her mum paused, not really looking at Lizzie. 'And *none* of this would have ever happened if…'

There was a moment's silence.

'If what?'

'You know what, Lizzie.'

'No!' Lizzie felt her eyes stinging, and stormed off through an open doorway.

*

Why does she still have to have a go at him? Lizzie thought, slamming the door behind her. *He's been dead over a year.* She leaned back against the door and closed her eyes, determined not to give in to tears. She could never imagine this hurt she felt subsiding. And she never wanted it to. *That would mean she'd stopped caring so much.*

When she opened her eyes again she noticed Mr Tubs had stolen through with her and she knelt down to hug him. He licked her cheek.

'Good dog.'

After holding him for a while, Lizzie stood up and turned on the light to get a better look at the room. It was a study, with floor-to-ceiling shelves of books lining the walls. There was an old, paper-strewn desk beneath a small window, and a tatty leather armchair facing a fireplace. In between the desk and the fire, a glass-panelled door led out into the darkening garden.

There were hundreds of books. Lizzie always used to run off and read whenever her parents argued – either in her room or, if it was warm enough, in the summer house in the garden. Back then, she only used to read adventure stories, but now she was increasingly reading her dad's old thrillers set in glamorous, far-off places. She was even persevering with some of his more serious books about ancient tribes and religions – the kind of books she and her mum used to tease him about.

Wiping away a tear – *how come her mum's tales about him still got to her?* – Lizzie walked over to the desk and picked up a book lying amid the papers. She read out the title: 'Hinduism – the Eternal Cycle.' The photo on the front was a statue of a dancing man with four arms, surrounded by a circle of flame. Definitely the sort of thing her dad would have read. *Perhaps this was why he was so intrigued by his wife's reclusive uncle.* She put the book down and peered through the grimy diamond-paned window into the garden. In the weak light she saw a paved walkway running alongside the house. Beyond the walkway was a semi-circular lawn with a sundial. The lawn was surrounded by a tall, curved hedge with a gap in the middle.

Lizzie glanced down and spotted a key in the glass-panelled door.

'Come on, Mr Tubs,' she said, turning the key and opening the door. The dog slipped between her and the doorframe, and ran off across the lawn.

As soon as Lizzie stepped outside she took a deep breath and felt her mood lift a little. All around, birds twittered in the hedges and trees. A large snail worked its way slowly across the sundial. The grass was long and wet, and the hedges ragged and overgrown.

Lizzie walked past the sundial to the gap in the hedge. She pushed through to see a grassy path heading down between more tall hedges, with openings on either side.

Intrigued, she walked forward and peered into the first gap. Beyond was a small enclosure, hemmed in by more dark hedges. An ornate iron chair stood alone on the untidy lawn, whilst three primitive-looking wooden heads gazed up from the far border. The small head was just taller than Mr Tubs, and the large one just shorter than Lizzie.

'Stop it!' said Lizzie, as Mr Tubs cocked his leg at the small one. The heads reminded her of the objects in the house.

She continued down the corridor, looking into each room-like enclosure. The next had an egg-shaped stone sculpture set amid a mass of silvery-leaved plants, and the one after a wooden monk standing between short, strongly-scented pines. Finally, before the corridor turned sharply to the right, there was a larger garden, divided in two by a dark-leaved bush.

The borders of this enclosure were littered with strange little statues – funny-looking men with the heads of animals, and cows adorned with flowers – but it was as Lizzie headed into the back section that she stopped and gasped.

Glowing mutedly in the grey afternoon light was a tall bronze statue of a man with four arms, dancing in a circle of metal flame. Dreadlocks like snakes flailed from his head, their tips welded to the ring of fire. The man's hips twisted, and one foot swung up to swipe the air. Beneath the other foot, a squat, miserable-looking dwarf gazed upwards, as if pleading for mercy.

The statue looked like the one on the front of the book...

In awe, Lizzie walked forward. She reached out and traced her fingers over the sharp flames. She peered at the burnished metal, and felt as if she was looking down into sunlit water. Then she stepped back and examined the man's face. His features – the smooth, blank eyes, narrow eyebrows, and thin mouth – were perfectly even. There was something both handsome and cruel in the symmetry.

After marvelling at the man for a moment, Lizzie looked down at the dejected figure on which he was dancing. She wondered what the poor thing had done wrong.

'Know how you feel, mate,' she said.

Suddenly Mr Tubs barked.

'What is it?' The dog started to jump up at the base of the statue.

'What?' said Lizzie, smiling.

'Lizzie! Where are you?' her mum shouted from the house.

For a moment Lizzie felt like keeping quiet, getting her own back by stressing her mum out; but then she shouted: 'Coming!' She beckoned to Mr Tubs. 'Come on, you,' she said.

The dog stood listening as she ran away, and down the grassy corridor. Only when he heard her back in the first garden did he sprint after her.

*

After exchanging muted apologies, Lizzie kindled a fire in the lounge whilst her mum cooked tea.

Like the hall, the lounge was filled with unusual pictures and ornaments, all covered in a layer of dust. Two small sofas faced each other in front of a tiled fireplace. At the end of the room a few steps led down into the kitchen, which had long windows giving views on to the drive and woods.

When the fire was going Lizzie's mum brought in beans on toast, with some juice for Lizzie and a large glass of wine for herself. They ate in silence, listening to the spit and crackle of the logs burning and the low rumble of thunder in the distance. Mr Tubs snored on the rug in front of the fire.

'We'll need to give this place a good clean tomorrow,' said her mum after a while. 'Chuck out some of this awful clutter.'

On the table beside her, in between a bronze sphinx and a ceramic dog, Lizzie spotted a picture of an old man with a long but well-trimmed white beard and a full head of white hair. She picked it up.

'Is this Great-Uncle Eric, Mum?'

Her mum glanced over. 'Yes.'

Lizzie studied the photo. *So this was the man who, for some strange reason, had left his house to a great-niece he'd never even met, stating she couldn't sell it until she was twenty-one.* He looked sharp and lively, not at all like the eccentric recluse her mum had described.

Didn't he have any closer relatives?

'He used to send me books on my birthday, didn't he?' she said, looking up at her mum.

'Yes – I'd forgotten about them,' said her mum, finishing her wine.

'Adventure stories, like "The Lion, The Witch, and the Wardrobe", and "The Secret Garden". I loved those books.'

'You've always loved reading.'

'What did he do?'

'He used to work at Bristol University. He was a Professor – of Anthropology.'

'That's ancient tribes, isn't it?'

'Sort of – but broader. The study of all humans.'

Lizzie took a moment to absorb this, then asked: 'Did he have a wife and kids?'

'No. Your gran said he had a big thing for a girl when he was young, but she died. Leukaemia or something. He lived the rest of his life on his own. Sad really...'

Lizzie looked up at the painting above the fireplace, which showed a stag with silver antlers standing before a knight riding in a dark forest.

'Stuck in the country, with nothing to do,' she muttered.

*

Whilst her mum was finishing her drink, Lizzie went upstairs and got ready for bed.

She had the smaller of the two bedrooms, at the far end of the landing. The room had a tiny window and a sloping ceiling. She liked the ceiling but the wallpaper was way too flowery. *She was going to need a lot of posters.*

When she was in her pyjamas, she sat down on the bed and opened her rucksack. In it was the beech photoframe she'd made in Mr Ahmad's class. She took it out and gazed at the picture of her dad on their holiday in Thailand, smiling and looking rugged in his white T-shirt. She remembered the fun they'd had, beachcombing and snorkelling whilst her mum spent the days lying in the sun. One day they found a dead snake, black and as long as Lizzie's arm, lying in the scrub at the edge of the beach. *It all seemed so long ago.*

She looked round at the cold, unfamiliar room and began to feel the ache of her grief coming back. As tears filled her eyes, she forced herself to remember how strong her dad had been. He would never have wanted her to cry – she had to be brave. But she just wanted him back. *Every bit of her wanted him back.*

She brushed at her damp cheeks, and put the photo on the bedside table. Then she pushed herself beneath the sheets, and switched off the lamp.

She lay awake for ages, listening to the distant thunder and letting her eyes adjust to the shapes in the darkness – a chest of drawers squeezed into an alcove, an old wooden chair, the thin, chequered curtain across the window. After a while she heard her mum come upstairs, creaking about on the floorboards as she used the bathroom and then went into her bedroom.

She heard an owl hoot, just before she fell asleep.

*

Something stirred her from her slumber. *Had Mr Tubs barked?*

As if on cue, another small *woof* came from downstairs, followed by silence.

Lizzie opened her eyes to see the room was bathed in moonlight. She sat up and drew the curtain.

Her eyes widened. The garden was bigger – *much* bigger – than she'd realised. The hedges outside the study carried on in a complex latticework, like a honeycomb, dividing the garden into many more sections than the ones she'd already seen. There was a glistening stream off to the right and, beyond that, a small, bright building with a pointed roof and single window.

She knelt and gazed at the garden in the moonlight, wondering what was in all the enclosures and the building. Then, just as she was starting to freeze, Mr Tubs barked again.

She realised her mum, a heavy sleeper, would never wake up, so decided to go and check he was all right herself. She climbed out of bed and pulled on her jumper and socks, then hurried downstairs.

But Mr Tubs wasn't under the stairs in the basket she'd made up for him.

Peering round in the gloom she saw the door to the study was open. She went in and found the sturdy little dog standing on a chair with his front paws on the desk. His nose was up against the window latch, as if he was trying to push it up.

'Mr Tubs – get down!' she said, striding towards him.

And froze, as a dark figure clutching a large bundle passed in front of the window.

The dog barked.

'Tubs!' Lizzie hissed, lurching forward and grabbing his mouth with both hands. She held her breath, expecting the sound of smashing glass as the man broke into the house. Instead, after a few moments, there was a crunching noise as feet headed off up the drive.

'Who was it?' she whispered in the dog's pricked ear.

Mr Tubs cocked his head and growled. Then he leapt out of her grasp on to the floor and pressed his nose against the glass-panelled door. He began to whine, and pawed the window pane.

'Shh! He might come back.' Was he a burglar? she wondered. *Neither her mum's nor her own phone had any reception, and the landline wasn't connected, so they couldn't call the police.*

Mr Tubs glanced back at her, and barked again. He seemed to want to go outside.

Lizzie's mind reeled. What should she do? She could go and wake her mum up. But what good would that do? *She'd only get hysterical.*

Mr Tubs kept whining, and scratching the door.

Perhaps it was just some local, taking a shortcut home through the garden?

'Stupid idea,' she muttered, then remembered her trick of thinking what her dad would have done.

Easy. He'd have gone out straight away, either to catch the intruder, or else to try and find out what he'd been doing. Perhaps he'd stolen something from the garden. *Some of those statues might be valuable.* She could wait and check it out in the morning – but then felt a rush of confidence. Why not go and look now, like Dad? *Especially as the man had gone – and she had a dog.* She ran into the hall and pulled on her trainers and coat. Then she came back and unlocked the door.

'Come on,' she said to Mr Tubs' eager little whiskered face. 'See if you can find out what he was doing.'

She opened the door and stepped out into the night. Mr Tubs darted around her legs and ran for the gap in the hedge.

'Hold on!' she said, sprinting after him.

The dog went through the opening and, followed by Lizzie, dashed to the end of the corridor. He disappeared into the garden with the dancing statue.

Panting, Lizzie stopped at the entrance and peered in. She glanced around the shadowy borders and the strange little statues, but couldn't see Mr Tubs.

Perhaps the man had stolen the statue of the dancer? *But it wouldn't have fitted in his sack.*

She wondered what she'd do if he came back – he might attack her! What was she doing out here like this? *Was she crazy?*

Suddenly she felt very scared. Where was Mr Tubs? Was he all right? *What if the man had an accomplice?* She crept across to the bush, noticing an unusual odour in the air – something almost metallic, rusty. Her heart thumped as she peered between the thick, waxy leaves into the back.

Mr Tubs was sitting looking at the statue of the dancing man, which shone softly in the moonlight. Otherwise, the garden was empty.

She scanned the dark corners of the hedges. Nothing. *There was no one there.*

Breathing a sigh of relief, she approached the statue, noticing the dramatic effect of the light on his stern features.

Mr Tubs barked.

'*Shut up!*' she whispered hoarsely, spinning round to check no one was jumping out at them from the bushes.

But instead of being quiet, Mr Tubs barked again. She ran at him and he leapt away, circling around the dancing figure. Furious at his yapping, Lizzie tried to catch him, but slipped on the damp grass. As she stumbled she reached out and grabbed the jagged rim of the statue.

And that's when it happened...

Chapter 2: Kashi

The statue and the dog and the garden began to blur. Overwhelmed with dizziness, Lizzie stopped and tried to steady herself. But instead the moonlight intensified, and suddenly it was adding colours, first the faintest of blues, and then violets and greens and before she knew it yellow and orange and by then all she wanted was to stop and she tried but couldn't and she felt the ground come up and a blackness come down, but a blackness that swirled with bizarre images of laughing elephants and monkeys and giant hairy-headed pigs with men's bodies brandishing spears, and then she had a sensation of something terrifying, an unseen presence that was dark and ruthlessly savage, before her awareness was snuffed out like a candle…

*

She opened her eyes into total darkness.

Where was she?

A wave of queasiness came over her, and she panicked as she realised she was trapped in a small dark space. Her knees were pressed up against her chest, and there was no light – at all.

Or so she thought, until she took a grip on herself and her eyes finally settled on the faintest smidgeon of greyness coming from somewhere off to the right.

Where was Mr Tubs? Where was the garden?

She wondered if she'd fainted, like when she was eleven and cut her hand with a saw making a jewellery box for her gran. Maybe she was out for the count, and dreaming.

She started to uncurl herself, intending to crawl towards the greyness. Immediately the floor gave way beneath her, and she splashed down into cool liquid. She staggered as she landed, grabbing at a rough wall behind her to keep herself steady. She clung to the wall, feeling sick and close to tears as her shoes and socks soaked through.

For a while, all she could think about was the most basic of things. She was Lizzie Jones, thirteen years old, on the short side of average for her age. She had hazel eyes that someone had once pleasingly called tawny, light brown hair kept up in a ponytail, and a nose still kinked from when she'd gone over her handlebars and smashed it. Whilst she'd lived most of her life in London she now lived in Rowan Cottage, near the village of Hebley, in Herefordshire. She had a new dog called Mr Tubs, who'd belonged to Eric Hartley, her eccentric great-uncle who'd died in his garden and left his house to her. She had moved to Rowan Cottage with her mum, Rachel, who smoked too much and never consulted her daughter on a single decision. And who claimed that Lizzie's dad, Robert, who died in a car accident a year ago in Scotland with his assistant Jane, had...

She must be dreaming. That was the only explanation. She must be dreaming about Mr Tubs and the intruder. Or maybe she'd slipped and banged her head whilst chasing Tubs around the statue. She felt a sudden chill, imagining herself lying unconscious in the cold garden. *Wake up!* she willed herself desperately.

But nothing happened. She was still there.

She shuffled forwards, heading towards the feeble light. Brittle objects shifted and crunched unpleasantly beneath her feet as she stepped through the water, and she struggled to keep her balance.

'Tubs?' she called timorously, just to hear the sound of her own voice. It was flat, as if she was in some kind of cave or tunnel. *Perhaps there was a sewer under the garden, with a manhole cover she hadn't noticed?*

The weak grey light emanated from an opening that gave access to another, smaller room, which ended in a flight of steep, gloomy steps heading upwards. She began to climb them. As she ascended, the light increased rapidly, and soon she spotted a bright blue rectangle above her – daylight! Floating on a sense of relief and unreality, she climbed up and out into the light.

And stopped, stunned, finding herself looking at the most extraordinary sight she'd ever seen.

An ancient sun-bleached city sprawled before her, stretched along the bank of an enormous river. The city's buildings were a bright, exotic mix of colours – red, ochre, sand, and white – and many had domes or intricate beehive towers. Some sat at the top of broad flights of steps that ran down into the water, whilst others were perched on the river's edge. A few tilted forward precariously, appearing as if they were about to collapse into the swirling waters and be lost forever. And everywhere, on the steps and in the buildings and out in small boats, the city's inhabitants went about their business in the soft, hazy sunlight.

Lizzie stood in awe, absorbing the view. *If only all her dreams were as impressive as this.* She looked down and realised she was standing on a narrow ledge that overhung the river a short drop below. Again she panicked, and grabbed hold of the wall. *What was she going to do?*

A few pigeons dropped from a nearby battlement, then swept across the water with a soft clapping of wings. Looking down, Lizzie saw a dark-skinned, middle-aged man in a loose white shirt rowing past in a boat. As he looked up his eyes met hers, fierce and direct, and she turned away, swallowing her fear. The man carried on up the river, slowly drawing his oars through the water.

She forced herself to concentrate, and turned to see that the small rectangular opening from which she'd emerged was at the bottom of a crumbling wall two or three storeys high. The ledge she was on was worn but stable, and carried on to both corners of the building.

She realised she had to do something, and decided to follow the ledge to the left, towards the main part of the city. But first, because the air was very warm – even though the sun seemed only just to have risen – she stripped off her jacket. Unable to think what to do with it – *she couldn't just leave it there* – she ended up clutching it against herself as she edged forward. Her waterlogged trainers squelched unpleasantly with each step.

The ledge turned the corner and ended in a broad walkway, in effect one giant step amid many smaller ones leading down to the river. All over the steps, people sauntered along in the warm morning light, or sat chatting in the shade of wooden umbrellas. Some stood at the river's edge or splashed about in the water, washing themselves. The women were flamboyantly dressed in bright headscarves and saris, whilst the men wore loose-fitting white clothes like pyjamas, or short-sleeved shirts and trousers. Some of the men down by the river were in various stages of undress, mostly with white or pink wraps around their waists. One was in his underpants, making Lizzie blush and look away.

'A dream. I'm dreaming,' she whispered. But it all felt so real – the heat of the sun on her skin, the loud, shouting conversations in a language she couldn't understand, the strong, slightly rank smell coming off the river...

She stepped off the ledge onto the pavement and started walking forward hesitantly. Her embarrassment grew as dark, earnest eyes followed her. Scared and confused, she avoided people's looks, and tried to keep her gaze fixed on the walkway in front of her. She became acutely aware of her oozing trainers.

A few steps down from her she noticed that one of the men in the river – a straggly character with a huge mop of black hair – was not, as she'd first thought, washing. Instead, he was cupping his hands and lifting some water up, straightening his arms, then opening his hands to let the water fall back into the river, whilst chanting something she couldn't make out. The man seemed to be addressing the sun, his eyes quivering but shut. After a moment he stopped, reached back on to the bank, and picked up a toothbrush and toothpaste.

He proceeded to brush his teeth using water from the river.

Yuck, Lizzie thought, hurrying on.

'Hey! Miss English!'

Shocked, Lizzie looked over to see a man in beautiful white robes and a turban, seated on a wooden platform beneath a large umbrella. He was near the river's edge, away from the other people. Around his neck was a bright orange cord.

'Me?' she said, glancing about to see if there was anyone else he could be talking to. Unsurprisingly, there were no other English girls around.

'Yes, you!' He smiled broadly at her. 'Come and sit with me. I will give you holy puja.'

It didn't sound like a particularly enticing offer but without knowing what else to do, Lizzie approached the man.

'Please – sit down,' he said, patting a small pink cushion in front of him.

'I can't…'

'Come on! Don't be scared. There's no money involved.'

His smile seemed so warm and welcoming Lizzie didn't feel she could decline. She sat down cross-legged in front of him, bundling her jacket in her lap.

'Now, tell me where you have come from.' The man was very handsome, with bronzed skin, white teeth, and dazzling golden eyes. He spoke in an Indian accent.

'Has the cat got your tongue?'

She realised she was staring blankly at him, up into his lovely eyes. For a second she felt like she'd believe anything they told her.

'Um – London – no, Herefordshire,' she said.

'London is a lovely city,' he said, smiling and rocking his head slightly from side to side. He picked up a necklace of carefully woven orange and yellow marigolds. 'Are you here with your parents?'

'No – on my own.'

'On your own? My, you backpackers get younger every year!' He reached over and hooped the necklace of flowers over her head, then evened it out around her neck.

Lizzie didn't know what to say, and dropped her gaze.

'So, you're from Herefordshire?' he said.

'Yes. Um – where am I?'

This time he laughed. 'Where are you? You are in Kashi, of course. Kashi the Luminous, City of Light. Beautiful Kashi, Shiva's city!'

She looked at him blankly.

'You probably know it as Varanasi,' he said, touching her arm. She certainly didn't. 'Banaras?' he suggested. Again, she was quiet.

The man bent forward, so his face was close to hers and their noses almost touching. He dabbed his thumb in a pot of red powder and pressed it on to her forehead, in between her eyebrows. Lizzie frowned, but didn't draw back.

'Never mind,' he said. 'I am Hanu, a brahmin, or *priest* as you would say, and I intend to give you the blessing of the Ganges, this most holy of rivers. You and your whole family will benefit most greatly. You must look at me all the time, look carefully at my eyes. The Lord God Shiva, the Holy Destroyer, imparts to you his deep blessing, with the Lord God Brahma, Creator of the Universe, and the Lord God Vishnu, Protector of the Universe. May the Holy Trimurti bring you eternal peace and release from samsara, the terrible cycle of suffering and rebirth…'

Lizzie started to feel like she was falling asleep, with the heat, the man's incandescent eyes, and the soft, brown river rippling behind him…

Suddenly an image of Tubs standing shivering in the dark garden popped into her mind.

'I have to go,' she said, shaking her head. The man's eyes seemed to lose their loveliness, becoming sharper, more fierce. The corners of his mouth tightened.

'Please stay,' he said.

'No, I have to go,' she repeated. 'Thank you for the flowers.' Hampered slightly by her bulky jacket she began to stand, pushing herself up from the cushion.

The man grabbed her wrist. 'No, wait,' he said.

She stood and pulled herself away, breaking free from his grip.

'Stay for the end of the blessing!' he said more loudly, rising to his feet.

Instead Lizzie turned and ran, away from the riverside and up the great steps into the ancient city.

'Come back!' shouted the man, but she was gone. He looked up at the crumbling building with the ledge, then pulled a mobile phone from under his robes.

*

Lizzie found herself in a narrow alleyway crammed with people.

It was hard to believe how many people there were. She saw young schoolgirls with satchels and bindied foreheads, weary men with white caps and sad eyes, scar-ridden beggars extending their palms upwards, bare-chested old men with knotted beards, and tearaway boys in dusty shirts. Everything was intense and uncomfortable, like the rush-hour tube in London, with everyone banging into each other and fighting to move amid the hot, pressing throng.

She pushed through them all, increasingly aware of the looks she was attracting. The panic she'd squashed down started to well up again. She kept her eyes down and carried on, thinking she had to get away from the strange man on the waterfront. In agitation she broke the marigold necklace and threw it to the ground.

The next moment the people in front of her swerved apart and she was left facing an enormous white cow, clopping heavily down the street towards her. She narrowly avoided being trampled by leaping into a doorway, and held her breath as the massive head and gentle brown eyes swung past without harming her. In a surreal moment, she noticed the cow also wore a garland of flowers around its neck. As she moved away from the door she spotted a small poster pasted to the wall, with a photocopied picture of a young boy surrounded by a very regular, non-English script. It looked like some kind of *Missing Persons* poster.

She hurried on through the crowd, trying not to make eye contact with anyone. At one stage she bumped into a gaunt-looking man with bloodshot eyes, who grabbed hold of her arm and held some cigarettes up to her.

'Want bidi?' he asked, but the look of horror on her face must have said it all, because he let go of her without another word and disappeared into the crowd.

Soon she emerged on to a broader, more modern-looking street, with a tarmac road, shabby concrete buildings, and a huge Pepsi billboard. The road was full of bikes, rickshaws, and small cream-coloured cars jostling chaotically for room to get by. The smell of burning oil choked the air, mixed with something worse – the sickly sweet odour of sewage.

Lizzie felt increasingly hot and disorientated. *She had to sit down.* Looking across the street she spotted a vegetable market, with a boy perched miraculously on a tall, neat pyramid of red potatoes. Beside him an old woman in a shawl was sorting fruit and a man was hawking what looked like blood on to the pavement. At the back of the market was a narrow, shaded area, towards which she made a beeline. When she reached the area she sat down on a concrete wall and checked her watch: 1:35. She put her face in her hands and tried to concentrate, but her mind felt like its sole occupant was a bucking donkey.

What was going on? This didn't feel like a dream. Shutting her eyes, she tried to disbelieve it, to focus her thoughts on her bed.

But the noise remained, the cacophony of car horns, revving engines, and people shouting. She pressed her face harder into her hands.

OK. She thought of sleep – deep, beautiful sleep, marshalling her off to a soft, empty space.

No. The noise and heat were still there. Again she felt panic rising.

'Hello.'

She looked up. Standing over her was a tall boy with a lean, wiry physique. He had aquiline features and large brown eyes. For an instant she was reminded of Japanese comics, in which the eyes were always drawn soft and big.

'I'm Pandu. What's your name?'

'Lizzie,' she said. Then added in desperation: 'Can you tell me where I am, please?'

'Varanasi, of course,' he said. The boy was dressed in a loose white collarless shirt, grey trousers, and flip-flops. His toes seemed to be ingrained with dust.

'Tell me I'm dreaming,' said Lizzie.

'You're dreaming,' said the boy, beaming at her.

'Not funny,' she said, scowling, and then added: 'You're just a part of my dream, right?'

'If you'll let me be.' Again he grinned, a broad, toothy grin, irrepressibly cheerful.

The grin made Lizzie even more irritated and she shook her head. 'I don't believe this,' she said, putting her knuckles back up to her cheeks. She stared at the ground.

The boy stood there for a moment watching her.

'Are you here with your parents?'

Lizzie didn't bother looking up. 'No. I mean, yes. They're down at the river.' She decided it was better to have parents around. *Safer.* 'My dad's an ambassador.'

'An ambassador? I'm impressed. Would you like to come and see my temple?'

'What?' She looked up again.

'Come and see my temple. It's dedicated to Ganesh. The God of Wisdom. Remover of obstacles.' She frowned at him. 'You look like you could do with some enlightenment,' he added, chuckling.

Lizzie didn't laugh. There was nothing she liked less than being patronised.

'Come on – you can meet the great Pharaoh Ramses the Fourth.'

'Pharaohs are Egyptian. This is supposed to be India, isn't it?'

'You're right, of course. But Ramses the Fourth is not Egyptian. He's Indian, born and bred. Most definitely, you can tell by the ears. Come on, I'll show you.'

'Holy Mother of God,' said Lizzie. It was an expression of her dad's she'd never used before, but it seemed to fit the situation perfectly.

Suddenly an idea struck her. She stood up and started walking back down the street, in the direction of the river.

'Hey! Where are you going?' cried the boy.

She ignored him and began to speed up.

'Hey!' he shouted. 'Come back!' He sped up alongside her, managing to dodge around most people, but unable to avoid knocking one man who cursed after him.

'Where are you going?' the boy repeated.

'None of your business.'

'Come and see my temple. I know you'll like it – there're loads of beautiful carvings and statues – all the tourists love it.' She felt his hand reach out and brush hers. She shook it away from him, still clutching her coat.

'Another time,' she said, and dived back into the narrow alleyway.

The boy stopped, watched her for a moment, then disappeared into a throng of tambourine-bashing pilgrims.

Lizzie's idea was that, by going back to the waterlogged room, she might be able to reverse the dream sequence and return to her own, waking world. She wondered whether she'd find herself lying in the cold Indian garden, Mr Tubs at her feet. Or maybe she'd still be in bed, having dreamt the whole thing.

She smiled to herself, reassured, as she came back on to the waterfront, which was now hot and dusty in the risen sun. She could imagine seeing herself from above, stirring as consciousness returned.

Relieved to see that the worrying priest, Hanu, was no longer sitting on his wooden platform, she hurried back to the ornate building with the ledge over the river. She edged her way around the walls to the rectangular hole and, with a sudden sense of trepidation – *what if it didn't work?* – descended the steep steps into the cool, watery chamber. She put her coat back on, allowing her eyes to adjust to the lack of light. Then she paddled awkwardly towards the back of the chamber, testing her footing before each step. Finally, her outstretched arms touched the far wall and she felt the rough alcove from which she'd dropped. She gripped the edge with both hands and hoisted herself back on to the ledge.

And screamed, as she felt herself plummeting downwards…

*

She dropped for what seemed like an eternity, before the swirling darkness was finally replaced by a rush of light, blue, yellow, violet, and green, like disco lights in her head, and the next thing the ground was hard and cold against her back and she was lying looking up at a night-time sky glinting with stars, and something wet and unpleasant was pushing across her cheeks...

Mr Tubs! She sat up and looked around.

She was back in the garden, the temperature was freezing, and it was dark. Mr Tubs was licking her face, then stepping backwards and forwards in excitement. She felt her head for bumps or cuts, and was relieved – if confused – to find none. *Her mum would go mad if she knew she'd been investigating an intruder in the middle of the night.*

She stood up and looked at the dancing statue, solid and inert.

It was all a dream. She must have slipped and knocked herself out briefly.

She shivered, suddenly feeling immensely tired. Her limbs ached and she yawned once, twice, and then again. *She had to get to bed.*

She hurried back into the house, locked the door, led Tubs to his basket under the stairs and ran up to her room, too exhausted to even consider the noise she was making. Throwing her coat on the chair, she kicked off her wet trainers and socks, and leapt into bed without removing her jumper.

Within seconds, she was asleep.

Chapter 3: Hebley

'Lizzie!'

She woke from jumbled images of suspicious looks, crazed holy men, giant cows, and barging, pock-marked women. The bedroom was suffused with light. Under the covers her jumper was all twisted around her, and she was sweating.

'Lizzie, are you still sleeping? Come on, you can't lie in bed all day.' Her mum poked her head round the door.

Lizzie looked at her wrist to check the time – but her watch wasn't there.

'What time is it?'

'Ten o'clock. You've been asleep for hours.'

'Ten?' She hardly ever slept that late.

Her mum came in and pulled the curtain. Instinctively Lizzie yanked up the bedspread to hide her jumper.

'We have to get this place cleaned up, and I'm not doing it all myself.'

Her mum bent down and peered at Lizzie's face. 'What's that?' she said. She licked her thumb, and wiped it between Lizzie's eyebrows. As it came away, Lizzie could see a pinkish smudge on it.

'Have you been at my makeup?'

She watched as her mum sighed and strode out of the room. Then she looked up wide-eyed at the sloping ceiling. Her mind flooded with memories from the night before.

What had happened?

She recalled everything so vividly. The intruder, going out in the garden, Mr Tubs' dance round the statue, the whirling colours, and the dark underground chamber. And everything that had happened afterwards in that strange city, the holy man, the cow, and the laughing boy. It all seemed so real.

She felt her wrist again. *Where was her watch?* She remembered the boy reaching out and touching her hand as she fled from him.

He must have stolen it. *He was a thief!*

But, if he'd stolen her watch, then the whole thing *was* real. But it couldn't be…

She fought back panic. There must be some rational explanation. Maybe she'd taken her watch off and put it down somewhere yesterday evening. *Or maybe she'd been sleepwalking.*

She sat up and looked out of the window.

The sky was a mix of blue and whitish-grey clouds. Patches of sun moved across the woods, which stretched away on all sides like a jumble of stags' antlers. Below, her great-uncle's garden was freshly bathed in sunshine. The tops of the criss-crossing hedges gleamed with reflected light. On the far side of the garden, the building she'd spotted was a small yellow tower, reached by a flagstone walkway. The walkway was lined with pedestals, and divided lengthways by a strip of water.

Looking at the lawn outside the study, Lizzie spotted the gap in the middle of the semi-circular hedge, with the corridor leading away. She could just make out the top of the dark green bush in the garden with the dancing man statue.

With a shudder, she crawled out of bed.

*

'Have you given that dog a bath, yet?' said her mum, coming into the kitchen.

Sitting with an untouched bowl of cereal in front of her, Lizzie glanced down at Mr Tubs, who thrust his nose into her palm. 'Mum…'

'Why don't you go out and do it in the garden? There must be a hose or something out there.'

'Mum, there's…'

'Ten-thirty,' said her mum, glancing at the kitchen clock and tutting. She headed back into the lounge, before Lizzie could say anything.

Lizzie stared out of the window, barely registering the blackened, mossy trunks of the wood. After a while she caught a waft of Tubs' coat. *Perhaps fresh air would help her think straight.* She went out of the kitchen door on to a patio and found a hose in a small outhouse. Tubs stood obediently still, shivering as she sprayed him with cold water. Slowly, her storm of confusion settled down.

She must have had a bad dream. A *really* bad dream. The pink on her forehead might have been blood from a small scratch she hadn't noticed. She'd probably put her watch on the bedside table and knocked it on the floor in the night. She would go upstairs and look for it as soon as she'd finished.

Everything else – the intruder, going out in the garden, the weird city – must have been part of the dream. She thought about the statue and remembered the book she'd seen on her great-uncle's desk.

Perhaps they had inspired the dream.

After she'd rubbed Tubs down with an old towel, she ran upstairs and looked under her bed. The watch wasn't there, but her old trainers were – *and they were damp.* With a shrinking feeling, she searched the rest of the room, then decided to go and look in the garden. As she came down through her great-uncle's study she spotted the book on Hinduism lying on the desk. She snatched it up and flicked to the central pages of black-and-white photographs. There were pictures of temples and stone statues of Indian gods, similar to the ones in the garden. When she turned to the final page and saw the last photograph, her mouth dropped open.

She was looking at a picture of the city she'd seen the night before.

Her stomach turned as she stared at the photo of the waterfront, with its broad flights of steps and higgledy-piggledy buildings. In this picture, dozens of men were praying in the shallow edges of the river.

Wide-eyed, she read the caption:

"It is believed that Hinduism has been practised in Kashi (also known as Benaras, and Varanasi) for over three thousand years. Here, in Shiva's City of Light, the Ganges is at its most sacred. Gurus come from all over India to worship on the ghats, *or holy steps."*

Powerful images from her dream began to come back to her. Feeling anxious, she hurried outside and retraced her steps through the hedge, scanning the path ahead. She reached the Indian garden, and hurried past the bush.

As soon as she saw the statue of the dancing man again, her stomach turned. She kept glancing up at his face as she kicked around in the grass, looking for the watch. She half expected to see him *do* something – to smile, frown, or turn his head slowly towards her. But his features remained fixed, and the only sound was Tubs snuffling around in the borders.

'It's not here, is it, boy?' she said, after a while. Tubs stopped rooting, and came beside her.

As she stood facing the statue she remembered her mum complaining about the odd conditions of her great-uncle's will. The reason it said Lizzie couldn't sell the house until she was twenty-one was so "she would have time to discover the garden's delights". Not the *house's* delights – the *garden's* delights. Her mum had dismissed it as the ramblings of a keen gardener – but was that all he'd meant?

With a sense of foreboding, another idea came into her head:

There was a very easy way to find out if it was all a dream...

The thought of touching the statue again made her crouch down and grab hold of Tubs for comfort. The little dog licked her face.

Lizzie tried to think of what her dad would have done in such an unbelievable situation. *He wouldn't have been scared.* In fact, he would have been excited. Really excited. For someone who travelled all over the world with his job, who loved going on foreign holidays, this would have been an amazing opportunity. He would have tried it again, to see what would happen.

Did *she* have the guts to do that?

*

As soon as she got back in the house her mum ushered her straight through the hall and out into the car, telling her they had to go shopping. As they drove through the tight country lanes Lizzie stared absently at the mountains in the distance, smooth as green velvet in the clear winter light.

'Not talking today?' said her mum.

Lizzie didn't know what to say.

'Fair enough…'

After a few minutes they reached Hebley, a small village of black-and-white cottages clustered around a sandstone church with a dark spire.

They parked by the village green. Three white geese stood on the grass with their heads up righteously, whilst a pair of mallards wheeled about on the surface of a small pond. Instead of following her mum straight into the Spar, Lizzie pulled her phone out of her pocket and checked for a signal. She felt desperate for contact with someone back in Croydon – back *home*. Despite only recently starting to make friends after changing school last year, she still longed for the sound of a familiar voice. But as usual, there was no signal.

She cursed and was about to follow her mum when she heard the clopping of horse's hooves. She turned to see a rider on a chestnut gelding coming down the centre of the road towards her. It took a moment to realise the broad, confident-looking figure on the horse's back was a woman, wearing a quilted olive jacket. A few strands of dark hair had come loose from beneath her helmet.

As the rider approached she beamed at Lizzie.

'Morning!' she called, drawing the horse up. 'Lovely day.' Her accent was strong and clear, foreign.

'Yes,' said Lizzie.

'Always nice to see a new face. On your hols?'

'No. We've just moved here.'

'Welcome. I'm Eva. Eva Blane. I live in the old Manor House.'

Lizzie smiled up at the woman. She had kind eyes – dark, but warm. *Her horse was gorgeous.*

'And... you are?'

'Oh. Lizzie – Lizzie Jones.'

'Where have you moved to?'

'Rowan Cottage?'

'Then you must be Eric Hartley's... granddaughter?' In one swift movement, Eva swung down out of the saddle and on to the road. Lizzie noticed her hand holding the cantle was bandaged.

'He was my great-uncle. Did you know him?'

'A little. He was a charming man.'

'Are you the Lady of the Manor?' At once Lizzie felt foolish. What a stupid... *hill-billy* kind of question. She was supposed to be from the Big City. *Grown up.* She turned to stroke the horse's nose, embarrassed.

'Well – I live in the Manor, if that's what you mean. But I don't have a title – not in this country, anyway.'

Lizzie's eyes widened. *Where did she have a title?*

'Where did you move from?' Eva asked.

'London – Croydon.'

'A bit of a culture shock!'

'Yes,' said Lizzie. Recalling her unbelievable night – or night*mare* – she added: 'It is.'

'So what are you going to be doing with your time?'

'Lizzie!' Lizzie's mum appeared from the shop. 'I wondered where you were.' She rushed up and grabbed Lizzie's arm. 'I hope she's not being a nuisance,' she said to the tall woman. 'She's obsessed with horses.'

'Mum!' Lizzie yanked her arm away, angry at being talked about as if she wasn't there.

'A fellow horse lover!' said Eva, looking Lizzie in the eye. 'Once you've settled in you must come to my stables. I've got a lovely pony I'm sure you'd like.

54

Doesn't nip like this one,' she said, smiling and showing her bandaged hand. Lizzie couldn't help wincing at the sight of some congealed blood showing through.

'If that's OK of course?' Eva added, turning to Lizzie's mum.

'Uh, well – maybe…' said Lizzie's mum.

'Anyway, great to meet you both,' said Eva, remounting. 'I'm having a party the day after tomorrow – just a few drinks in the afternoon, from two. You're welcome to come.'

'Great!' said Lizzie.

'Well… we have a lot of things to do – but thanks for the invite,' said her mum.

As Lizzie was drawn away she threw a glance back at Eva, who gave her a quick, confiding smile.

*

After lunch, Lizzie went out into the garden with Mr Tubs. As soon as she was alone her head began to spin, thinking about the previous night. *Had she really spent a couple of hours in India?* It was impossible to believe. It was a dream. But say, just for a moment, she pretended it wasn't – *was it really that awful?* Whilst everything had been bewildering at the time, nothing bad had happened to her. And she'd been able to get back easily when she'd worked out how. Perhaps she could try going round the statue again? *Just to make sure it was a dream.*

'I can't believe it. I can't believe what I'm actually thinking,' she said to Tubs. 'Have I gone mad?'

But as she followed the rambling yew corridors, she became increasingly distracted by the garden itself. There was so much of it, with every twist and turn of the corridors revealing a new view, or a garden *room* full of sculptures overgrown by moss. She found a herb garden, measured out by little bay trees like lollipops, a woodland area, concealing a stagnant, overhung pond, and a lavender garden, with an open summerhouse. There were mosaics, carvings and statues of all shapes and sizes, bright and drab, large and small, wood, metal, and stone, each displayed in its own special area. She wondered where her great-uncle had got everything from.

Heading towards the small tower, she came to the biggest enclosure, which was empty except for a row of pruned trees leading to a large granite block. From the top of the block, an angel gazed demurely at the lawn.

There were words carved into the granite:

EVELYN HARTLEY: 1895-1994

"The Spring"

I journeyed far
Before I saw
In darkness, light
In truth, lies
And, in one place –
The Fountainhead –
All

The poem didn't seem to be finished. *All what?* Lizzie wondered whether this was the grave of her great-uncle's mother or sister. *Which would make her… Lizzie's Great Grandma, or Great-Aunt.*

The sun was beginning to set as she finally made her way to the yellow building. She walked up the flagstone path between the water channel and tall hedges, stepping around the empty pedestals. At the top of the channel was a plinth with a man's face carved into it. The water for the rill was pouring from the man's open mouth, over a mass of ivy leaves and tendrils – both engraved and real. Plants also crept out of the man's hair and ears, reminding Lizzie of the strange plastercast in her great-uncle's hall.

She studied the face and shuddered, as if something had brushed the back of her hair. As she reached up to feel her ponytail, everything seemed to turn darker. She looked up to see if there was a cloud, but the sun was still clear, and the light the same. Thinking there was something distinctly odd about the face, she hurried on to the more welcoming, primrose-coloured building.

An arched door in the side of the tower opened to reveal a storage room with tools and flower pots, and a small rickety staircase going up. At the top was a room with bare floorboards and a few pieces of old furniture, including an armchair with a torn red cushion, and a table in front of the solitary window. A single bed with a bare mattress was set along one wall.

Lizzie wondered whether her mum would let her stay down here with Mr Tubs. The room was cold and damp now but, as the weather improved, she could imagine herself sitting in the armchair reading whilst the small dog lay curled at her feet. *It could be their own special den.*

She looked through the window and saw the water channel, now flashing brassily with the setting sun. On the table were a few scattered sheets of yellowed paper. She picked them up and glanced through them. They were mainly sketches of plants, except for one which was a hand-drawn map of the garden with the names of each room neatly inscribed in blue ink. The garden outside the study was called the Sun Garden, and the one with the dancing statue was – predictably – the Indian Garden. She skimmed the names quickly: Easter Island, The Rainbow Serpent, Inca Garden, The Edwardian Path – the list went on. The building she was standing in was simply called The Tower, and the spewing statue was the Fountainhead. One garden with a large tree was known as Miss Day's Garden. She wondered who Miss Day might have been, smiling as she imagined an energetic Victorian spinster in cotton gloves with a passion for peonies.

She looked up as the last streak of sun was vanishing on the horizon. She took a moment to admire the garden from her new vantage point, watching the golden-green hedge tops misting with the cold. She felt giddy, remembering the crazy dream but also scarcely able to believe that all this was *hers*.

'It's gorgeous,' she whispered to Mr Tubs who, after a precarious little jump, had managed to perch on the windowsill and look out too.

The dog barked, as if in agreement.

*

That night, as soon as she thought her mum was asleep, Lizzie crept downstairs, tugged on her coat and trainers, and headed out into the garden with Mr Tubs.

There was a light breeze, and the air was cold. Tubs was wearing a little quilted jacket she'd dug out from under the stairs, but he still gave the occasional shiver as he trotted along beside her.

The moon was obscured by clouds, but there was just enough light from the stars for her to make her way to the statue of Shiva in the Indian garden. She knew now who it was because she'd spent the evening reading the book on Hinduism in her great-uncle's study. Shiva was one of the three main gods of Hinduism, the other two being Brahma and Vishnu. Lizzie remembered the priest Hanu – *in her dream, of course* – mentioning them all. Brahma was the creator of the universe, Vishnu was its protector, and Shiva was its destroyer. But he wasn't its destroyer in a totally negative way, because by clearing things out he made way for new things to grow and flourish. Lizzie liked that idea. The statue in the garden depicted him in one of his classic poses as Lord Nataraja, dancing on the demon of ignorance and fear. She liked that too.

Her reading had reinforced her curiosity, which had finally overcome her anxieties and doubts. By the time her mum had told her to go to bed she was feeling increasingly courageous, and determined to find out whether it was real.

But as soon as she was standing shivering in front of the statue's impervious bronze face she felt herself withering.

Was she really going to try it again? *What if it worked?*

Then she thought of her dad, and told herself not to be such a coward. *She had to know.*

'Here goes, Mr T,' she said, grabbing hold of the rim of flame and starting to step around it.

It worked! *All of a sudden colours were breaking out from the fabric of the night, from ultraviolet into bright reds and yellows and greens, and then into all the colours of the rainbow, and her weight seemed to fly away from her feet and tumble all around her body as if she was in some kind of cosmic washing machine. For a moment it felt as if she was in space, out in the deep, dark blue with stars glimmering all around her, surrounded by those strange half-human, half-animal presences again, and then she tried to keep her eyes open but everything went black...*

And again she came round in cooped-up darkness, her knees pressed up against her chest, with only the dimmest light filtering in through the far doorway.

This time the sense of disorientation passed away more quickly. As soon as she felt confident to move, she took her shoes and socks off and lowered herself down into the shallow water. Then, instead of going out, she leapt straight back into the hole.

The process reversed successfully and within moments she was on her back in the garden with Mr Tubs lying beside her, sniffing her ear.

It was real!

She could scarcely believe it. How did it work? *It was like something out of Star Trek, like one of those teleporters.*

Her great-uncle's words came back to her: ...*time to discover the garden's delights...*

He must have known about it. She thought about the books he'd sent her when she was younger, in which children were always having amazing adventures through magical gateways they'd discovered in strange houses – or strange *gardens*. The books must have been a small signal, a way of starting to prepare her for this. Was the world *really* a more magical place than most people ever realised, with only a few lucky enough to find it out?

In the midst of her euphoria she remembered the intruder. Was this why he'd come into the garden? Her mind boggled for a moment.

Then, with a sudden burst of confidence, she ran around the dancing Shiva, keen to see again his city – Kashi, the City of Light...

Chapter 4: The Pisaca of Kashi

For several weeks now, Jatinder had been getting up well before dawn.

Dhani the boatman had a new strategy for hooking in those backpackers who weren't part of a package holiday, or who hadn't been cornered by rickshaw wallahs the night before. The strategy was simple enough. Jatinder acted as a roving salesgirl, circling the main hostels from five until seven a.m. When the bleary-eyed Swedes, Brits and Israelis came out, she would ask them if they were planning a dawn boat trip to see the magnificent ghats and temples in what was universally acknowledged to be the best light. Invariably they were, since there was no other reason for them to be getting out of bed at such an unearthly hour. Jatinder would then hit them with the sales pitch.

Being tall for her age, with long dark hair and a lively intelligence, she was particularly good at talking the young men round. She knew lots of them found her pretty, and used it shamelessly to her advantage.

Sometimes she earned hundreds of rupees in a morning – a fortune in comparison to her previous job as a maid for a destitute brahmin family out in the suburbs.

This morning had been going well. Jatinder had nearly filled one boat load, persuading a group of three Swedish boys and an Austrian girl to wait for Dhani in a cafe, as he hadn't been around and she guessed he'd overslept again. She was particularly pleased with herself, as the backpackers could have easily taken another boat, there were plenty around. But she'd convinced them that Dhani was not only the cheapest but the best, as being in his forties he knew so much more about the history of the ghats than the younger boatmen. She'd neglected to tell them that, also because of his age, he could only take them half as far.

Thinking she could find another couple of travellers to fill the boat if she was quick, she headed up into the cramped, residential quarters behind Dashashwamedha ghat.

The sun hadn't yet crept above the horizon, and the narrow back streets were still filled with shadows. Jatinder made her way towards a hotel called The Paris that she rarely visited, tucked away near a small, ancient fountain square. She passed a pair of old men drinking their first cups of chai outside a tiny cafe, and then turned down a long, empty alley, strung across with washing.

About half way down the alley she heard a noise behind her and looked around. Someone had appeared at the end of the alleyway and was following her. From the figure's shape and size it appeared to be a woman, but there was something odd about her. At first Jatinder thought she was dressed entirely in black – perhaps a Muslim, wearing the niqab veil. But then, as she glanced around again, she realised the woman's figure was too well-defined for her to be in the long veil. In fact, as she looked more carefully, she realised that the woman was not dressed at all – she seemed to be naked. It was her skin that was so dark.

At that moment Jatinder felt the temperature drop, and something happened to the air around her. Everything seemed to flash black and silver – like the afterimage on an eye which had briefly glimpsed the sun – before returning to its normal hue. But something intangible, a sense of underlying disturbance, remained in the alley.

What was someone doing naked in the streets of Kashi? Jatinder wondered nervously. Her scalp began to crawl as she remembered the stories which had been flying around the city of the terrible child killer - *the Pisaca of*

Kashi. Until now, like most kids, she'd shrugged them off with bravado.

When she next looked back she noticed that not only had the strange, black-skinned woman gained on her, but she'd also been joined out of nowhere by two more. The women were advancing on her speedily, and one was making a deep, guttural noise, like a lioness chasing down prey.

Jatinder fled.

She leapt over rubbish and open drains and dived down passageways, making her way towards the fountain square where she hoped to find other people. Behind her, she could hear the women giving chase, easily matching her speed and lightness of foot. She began to fear for her life and shouted for help. But no one came, nor even looked out of a window.

Finally, she turned into a street that led up to the square and felt a huge sense of relief to see an old woman, crouched in a doorframe.

'Help, please help!' she shouted, as she ran towards the figure. The crone, dressed in a dark cloak and shawl, was looking the other way. As Jatinder drew up to her, she glanced back and noticed that the women had disappeared. She breathed a sigh of relief.

'What is it?' asked the bent woman in a thick, gravelly voice, her face still turned away.

'I – there were some strange women chasing me back there – but they've gone now,' said Jatinder, her eyes welling with tears. 'They weren't wearing any clothes and they had really black skin.'

'Black? Like obsidian?' said the woman. Something in the tone of her voice made Jatinder think she might be mocking her. She wondered why the old woman hadn't looked up.

'Who… who are you?' asked Jatinder.

Suddenly a taloned hand shot up and grabbed her wrist, pulling her down sharply.

Jatinder didn't have time to scream.

*

The thought of seeing Hanu again made Lizzie's skin crawl, so she followed the ledge around the other way this time. The large steps – *ghats*, the book called them – ran down into swathes of greyish mud on the other side. A bearded man and two teenage boys were wading in the silt with their trousers rolled up, wobbling about and joking with one another. Sitting near them on the lowest ghat was a plump woman in a sequined ivory dress and headscarf. A magazine was open on her lap, but instead of reading she was watching the boys and laughing.

Unseen by the small group, Lizzie jumped off the ledge on to the steps and climbed upwards. The ghats

were very steep here and halfway up she came across
three black-and-white mountain goats perched on the
steps, as naturally as if they were on a cliff. One of
them munched a chunk of cabbage as Lizzie clambered
past it, a rueful expression on its face, whilst the other
two gazed impassively out across the sleepy brown
river.

Once again Lizzie entered the frenetic network of
passageways that led away from the ghats. More
confident this time, she watched people for longer,
even when her gaze was fiercely returned. Every face
she saw was fascinating, etched with its own
unfathomable story. Many people looked wretchedly
poor and desolate, and she couldn't help flinch as she
spotted beggars – including several children – with legs,
eyes, or hands missing. But others seemed wealthier,
clean-shaven men with neatly-pressed white robes and
caps, and self-assured young women with embroidered
saris and lustrous hair.

Everywhere she looked she found temples and
shrines. Some were magnificent buildings with grand
arches leading to sumptuous interiors, whilst others
were little more than tiled concrete shelters housing
red-spattered effigies. There were temples dedicated to
gods she'd seen as statues in the garden, some of which
she'd been reading about during the evening: boar-

headed Vishnu, monkey-headed Hanuman, and blue-skinned Shiva, the Lord of Destruction. Most thronged with activity, with bearded, half-naked priests lighting incense, barefoot attendants lovingly scouring cracked tiles, and vendors hawking garish portraits of blue deities. But some were deserted, and she wondered dreamily if these were for gods who'd been forgotten.

The other thing she noticed as she walked about were the strong, pervasive odours, ranging from the pleasantness of jasmine and spices, to ghastly wafts of sewage, and fruit left out to rot in the heat. The roads, cluttered with cars and motorised rickshaws, reeked of oil and diesel.

As she roamed the streets she kept imagining how proud her dad would feel if he was watching her. *His 'little big girl' was truly grown up now.* At one stage she noticed an old woman looking at her strangely, and realised she had a huge grin on her face.

After wandering about for an hour or so, Lizzie noticed a new smell – burning. Curious, she headed in the direction of the smell and found herself coming back towards the river. Soon she spotted white smoke, billowing from one of the lower ghats. As she tried to get nearer, her route was blocked by a fence. Several people were peering over, including two middle-aged tourists in khaki breathables and baseball caps, with cameras around their necks.

As she came up beside them she realised that one of the Indians, a short man with a neat parting, was talking about the area below.

'… the famous Manikarnika Ghat and Kund, where it is said that he who is cremated is released from *samsara*, the cycle of reincarnation, thanks to the blessing of Lord Shiva whose presence permeates the very air of the city.…'

Lizzie pushed up on tiptoes to peep over the fence. Strewn across the ghats below she saw two large bonfires blazing away, tended by dark, sweaty men in loincloths. Lined up at the water's edge on wooden stretchers were a few corpses in white and orange shrouds. As she watched, two of the skinny, troubled-looking men came and lifted one of the stretchers and bore it to a point just above the nearest fire. They then proceeded to hoist it directly on to the flames. Lizzie watched in amazement as corpse and stretcher burned fiercely in the intense yellow heat.

'That's incredible,' said the white woman, in a harsh, North European accent. She was short and stocky, with cork-screwed grey hair springing out from the sides of her baseball cap. Her whole face was beaded with sweat.

'For us, the Ganges here is at its most sacred,' said the guide. 'The remains of the body will be thrown in the water, thus guaranteeing an end to earthly suffering.'

Lizzie looked at the river. There was a dead buffalo, its bloated flank like the head of a whale, drifting slowly downstream.

'No, please don't!' she heard the guide exclaim.

She looked round to see that the male tourist had lifted his camera and was about to take a picture. The other Indians were staring at him angrily. As the shutter clicked, one of the men snatched the camera out of his hand and hurled it on the ground.

'Hey! What do you think you're doing?' shouted the tourist. He was broad and overweight, with layered jowls and bright pink skin. He grabbed the Indian by the arm and raised his fist as if to strike him.

The guide dived between them and began shouting at the Indian in what Lizzie guessed was Hindi. A heated exchange took place, as the two tourists backed off. After a few moments the man who'd snatched the camera shouted something final, glared at the tourists, then stormed away.

The guide picked up the camera and handed it back. It was a professional-looking Nikon, and the lens had cracked.

'I am very sorry,' he said. 'But I told you this ghat is sacred and that photography is forbidden here.'

The tourist scowled. 'Come on,' he said to his wife. 'We're going.' They headed back up the ghats, into the city.

'What about my payment?' shouted the guide.

'That'll cost me a hundred Euros to repair,' said the man, without looking round.

The guide cursed in Hindi, then turned and caught sight of Lizzie. He fixed her with an intense stare, ablaze with anger, then hurried off up the ghat.

Feeling disconcerted, Lizzie decided it was time to head home. She made her way back down a quieter street, passing solitary women trying to sell meagre portions of fruit and vegetables in doorways. The women watched her sullenly as she passed, and she realised the depth of their poverty – and how rich she must seem to them, in her smart trainers and jeans. She knew the hard differences between rich and poor kids at home – the vicious insults you'd get, just for wearing the wrong label – but she'd never experienced the divide of wealth as acutely as here.

Suddenly, the sharp two-tone blare of a siren sounded up ahead. She noticed a crowd was gathering at the end of the street in a small square. There was a fountain in the middle of the square, but it was hard to see much else due to all the people. When she finally squeezed in, she heard a couple of anxious policemen in brown uniforms yelling at everyone.

Then, as one onlooker moved aside, Lizzie caught sight of the upper torso of a teenage girl, sprawled face down at the base of the fountain. There was some dark stuff – *surely not blood?* – soaking into the ground, almost indistinguishable from the child's long dark hair.

Lizzie froze, as more people pushed in and again obstructed the view. All the time the square was filling with people, flooding out of doors and alleys. Upper floor windows swung open, and women and children leaned out to get a better look.

As Lizzie fought back an urge to be sick, there was a sudden commotion at the front of the crowd. A scrawny old man with a waist-length beard broke through, bellowing loudly and swinging a staff. The man was dressed only in a loincloth, and his skin seemed to be caked with chalk or ash. Red lines were daubed across his nose and cheeks, adding to his haunting appearance.

As soon as the man broke through the police cordon, an officer ran forward with his arms out, pleading with him to go back. The old man – who Lizzie thought must be some kind of holy man – pushed him out of the way, and strode towards the

73

prostrate child. He bent down and turned her over, but then Lizzie's view was blocked again by someone in front of her. The last thing she saw was a strange look of... *relief*... on the priest's face, which was quickly replaced by anger.

'Excuse me, young lady! Where are your parents?'

Lizzie looked up to see a portly young policeman standing beside her. He was well-groomed, with short, wavy hair and smooth, babyish skin. Pips on his sleeve made Lizzie think he must be an officer.

'Um – they're down on the ghat,' she lied.

'You can see, a child's been killed here,' he said, sounding like someone from one of the black-and-white films Lizzie's gran used to watch in the afternoons.

'How did she die?' asked Lizzie.

'It was murder,' said the policeman. 'A very brutal murder, I'm afraid. I'll take you back to your parents now. It's not safe round here. What's your name?'

'Lizzie – Lizzie Jones,' she said, wondering how she could escape.

'I'm Inspector Farruwallah. You can call me Raj. Now, come on – show me to your parents.'

'It's OK. I can find them. Don't worry.'

'No, I insist.'

She led him back down the alleyway and into an unpaved passage that sloped sharply downwards.

'You must stay with your parents at all times,' said the Inspector as they walked. 'Several children have been murdered in the last few months. There's a killer on the loose. *The Pisaca of Kashi*, or the Cloaked Demon, as some say. Huh! Pisacas! Fairytales, of course. But as you can see, the killer is very real, and you have to be careful. You mustn't go out on your own again.'

But Lizzie was barely listening to him. She noticed a narrow passageway coming up on the left, just before the buildings gave way to the dazzling silver-blue light of the sky and river. As they drew up alongside the passageway she darted sideways into it, and started to run as fast as she could.

'Hey! Come back!' the policeman shouted.

He pursued her for a while but soon she emerged into a crowded street, where she managed to disappear amid the throng of people, bikes and rickshaws. She headed back to the disused temple overhanging the river.

*

Back in the garden, Tubs had been sitting waiting patiently for her beside the statue. He leapt up when she reappeared.

'Tubs – you look freezing,' she said, kneeling down and giving him a big hug. She felt tears in her eyes, and knew they were from more than just the cold.

'Come on,' she said, 'let's go back inside.'

Soon they were back in the study, which still felt warm from the fire Lizzie had lit earlier. She took the little dog in front of the embers and, sitting down on the rug, began to rub his sides through his padded coat. His haunches continued to shiver sporadically.

'Sorry, boy,' she said. 'Sorry…'

She couldn't stop thinking about the murdered girl. Visions of the bloodstained body kept flashing through her mind. What with the reality of the portal itself, it was too much to take in.

She was sitting in a sick haze when Tubs' ears pricked and he ran to the glass-panelled door. Hearing the dull thud of footfall on the path, she quickly crouched down as a moonlit figure strode past the window, heading towards the kitchen and the drive.

This time the intruder's hood wasn't up, and Lizzie saw that it wasn't a man at all, but rather a woman with a pale, white face and long, frizzy hair tied up at the back…

Chapter 5: The Feral Child

The next morning Lizzie could hardly open her eyes when her mum banged on the door to wake her.

Yawning repeatedly, she swung herself out of bed and shuffled through to the bathroom. All the outrageousness of the night – the reality of the portal, the murder, the woman's appearance in the garden – came back as she stood under the fitful, none-too-hot shower.

What was she going to do?

'Now, I'm going to do the kitchen and I want you to clean your bedroom today. Polish all the surfaces – including the window sill – and vacuum the carpet. The hoover's in the cupboard under the stairs,' her mum began, as soon as Lizzie came into the kitchen.

'Mum…'

'What?'

'Can't we have a break?'

'No, we can't. Clean your room. Then – and only then – you can take that dog out for a walk. I don't want you disappearing off like yesterday.'

Lizzie thrust her head down at the cereal bowl. She felt as if she could do with a break from *everything*.

'You haven't been staying up late reading, have you?' said her mum. 'You look tired.'

'No.'

Things might be bad, confusing – unbelievable, even – but there was no way she was talking to her about *anything*.

*

'Real, real,' Lizzie kept saying later as she walked through the woods, Tubs snuffling in the undergrowth behind her. 'It was *real*.'

She'd always envied her dad's geology trips abroad for his company, and now she could go to *India* whenever she wanted... But her momentary elation was cut short as an image of the dead girl's body flared in her mind. *How could anyone do that to a kid?*

Whilst she felt certain her great-uncle had known about the portal – and, for some reason, wanted her to know about it too – she wasn't sure she could deal with it. Especially now she'd discovered there was a murderer on the loose.

But... what was the woman with the frizzy hair doing? Was she using the portal too?

And, if so, why?

Her mind spinning, Lizzie looked up to see she'd reached the edge of the wood. She gazed across the fields towards a distant hill. Immediately she spotted a boy cycling aimlessly about on the path. As soon as he saw her, the boy began pedalling towards her. She recognised him as the son of Mrs Bennett – *Thomas.* When Lizzie and her mum had arrived to collect Mr Tubs he'd kept his distance, skulking around at the edge of the farmyard. His mum had had to introduce him.

Now, Thomas slewed to a halt in front of her and dropped his bike sideways between his legs, as if to block the path. Mr Tubs bristled and stepped forward, like a mini guard dog.

'Hi,' said Lizzie.

Thomas grunted something that could have been a greeting. Then he said: 'Are you one of them?'

'What?'

'You look like you're one.'

'One what?'

'One of the witches.'

'What?'

But instead of answering, Thomas looked off towards the horizon. Then he said: 'Heard about the wild kid living in the woods?'

'No.' Lizzie was wondering how she could politely scat. Thomas was evidently a nutter, which was all she needed right now.

'Leanne Stykes from the Spar was woken up by a noise in the night,' Thomas continued. 'She pulled the curtains and there was this little gypo kid, going through the bins. He scarpered when he saw her.

'Now Dad's worried there might be a whole caravan coming, like the year before last. But I've got another theory.'

Lizzie didn't say anything. Thomas drew in a deep breath and then said: 'You know what Wicca is, don't you?'

'Yes,' said Lizzie. 'It's witchcraft.'

With a hint of satisfaction in his eyes, Thomas said: 'There's been witches round here for centuries, and they're still round now. They do spells in the wood. Black magic. Curses that make you're your hair fall out or give you cancer, if they hate you enough. I know, I've seen where they do it.

'I reckon this is a kid they've kidnapped and tried to sacrifice. To Pan or someone.'

Lizzie snorted. 'Sounds like something from a fairytale.'

'You wouldn't think so if you knew what I knew. You wanna know something else?'

'What?'

'Your uncle was one of them – just like you!'

Lizzie struggled to conceal her shock. 'What you on?' she said.

She began to turn back towards the woods but stopped, as the thin sound of a horn came across the fields. She looked towards the hill and spotted a pack of dogs, followed by riders in blue coats, bursting from a copse.

'Hunters!' she said.

'Yeah,' said Thomas. 'That'll be Godwin Lennox and co.'

'But it's against the law!'

'Won't stop 'em round here.'

'That's terrible!'

'Country ways, my dear,' he said, affecting a mock-refined accent.

Lizzie's anger at being referred to as Thomas's *dear* didn't have time to fully materialise as she caught sight of the orange streak of the fox, speeding down the hillside. Behind it the dogs, brown-and-white beagles, bayed as they chased the scent.

'Come on!' Lizzie yelled at the fox. 'I'm going to report them...'

Thomas snorted. 'A lot of good that'll do. Godwin's like that with the Chief of Police,' he said, holding up crossed fingers.

The next thing that happened was even more bizarre. As the fox came down along the field two women jumped up from a ditch close to the dogs, and started shouting and banging small drums. One was elderly and the other was tall, with bright, auburn hair tied up at the back of her neck. Their drab cloaks had helped to camouflage them.

'Sabbers!' said Thomas, gleefully.

The women's actions confused the beagles, but not for long. After a few moments of indecision, they continued to bear down on the fox.

Then what Lizzie was dreading happened.

The two leading dogs reached the fox, and began snapping at its legs. After a couple of failed lunges, one of them caught hold of the exhausted creature and all three crashed into the mud in a struggling mass of fur.

'No!' shouted Lizzie. A vision of the dead Indian girl flashed in her mind. She began running across the field with Mr Tubs.

But as soon as the fox went down the whole pack piled in on top of it, quickly tearing it to pieces. Stunned, Lizzie stopped and looked away.

The hunters slowed as they passed the younger woman. Lizzie saw one of them – a middle-aged man with silver-grey hair and glasses – raise his whip at her threateningly. The old woman stepped in between them and shouted something Lizzie couldn't hear.

She was still shouting as Lizzie came closer.

'I'll have you for assault!'

The silver-haired man laughed at her, then wheeled his horse and headed off with the rest of the hunters towards Hebley, the dogs trotting beside them.

'How could they do that?' said Lizzie.

'They're animals,' said the old woman, shaking with anger.

'And half the bloody police are in with them,' added the auburn woman. She stepped forward and stared down at Lizzie and Tubs. She had very clear green eyes. Patches of mud on her cheeks made her look like some kind of Celtic warrior.

'That's a special dog you have there,' she said.

Lizzie looked at Tubs, who was looking up at the woman. 'What… what do you mean?' she said.

'He's clever. Truly his master's dog. You look after him.'

Then, with a burst of panic, Lizzie recognised the tall, cloaked woman.

She was the intruder.

Lizzie stumbled back a couple of steps.

The woman stared at her for a moment, and then said to her elderly companion: 'Come on, Madeline – let's go.'

And then the two were trudging away across the fields, back towards Hebley.

Lizzie experienced a wave of dizziness. She felt overwhelmed, out of place.

'Out of your depth now, aren't you, townie?'

It was Thomas, coming up behind her on his bike. She didn't look around, afraid he might see the tears welling in her eyes.

'Scared of the witches?'

'What?' She looked askance at him, hoping her fringe would hide her tears.

'That was two of them. Madeline Kendall, and Ashlyn Williams. The ones I told you about, who did sacrifices in the woods with your great-uncle, el freako…'

'Get lost!' Lizzie cried.

The boy made a sarcastic *oooh!* as he cycled past her. She could hear him laughing as he raced away.

As soon as Lizzie was back in the wood, she leant her head against her forearm on a tree and began to cry. Mr Tubs looked up at her in watery-eyed concern.

*

Lizzie and Thomas had not been the only ones watching the terrible culmination to the hunt.

Up in the rickety second storey of the barn a small boy with brown skin, dusty hair, and a dark cut on the side of his head sat shivering in filthy clothes, peering from the corner of a window.

The boy saw the band of blue-coated *Raksasa* go pounding by on their mounts, chasing the poor fox-spirit with their dogs. He peered anxiously amongst them and was relieved to see no sign of the *Pisaca*. He saw the boy riding slowly about on the bike, and the girl with the pony tail who'd emerged from the trees with her dog.

The boy watched everything, trying to control his feverish breathing. The anxiety of the hunt brought back memories of the night before – *of the priest disappearing into the river, and of the face, the terrible face of the Pisaca, which had been the last thing the he saw before he woke in the dark room... in which, miraculously, after scrabbling around for hours, he'd found an open grid, small enough for him to squeeze through and escape out into this cold land...*

The sight of the two women leaping up in the field and shouting at the dogs brought him back to the present. His head swam with amazement when the tall women beat her drum, like a warrior from the *Mahabharata*, fearlessly drawing the attention of the Raksasa to herself. He wondered at the women's courage, the way they appeared to have no fear for their lives. Perhaps they weren't real flesh, maybe they were ghosts or immortals. Maybe they couldn't be killed like him, a mere boy.

Then the boy twisted his head away as the ravenous hell-dogs fell upon the fox and tore it apart. He prayed that the poor beast wasn't the *vahana* of a god, that it was simply a creature of this Earth.

Or whatever freezing hell he'd found himself in.

*

Had the woman with the auburn hair used the portal?

As Lizzie came back down the drive with Tubs to the cottage, she felt a sudden chill remembering the Indian policeman's words: '*The Pee*-something... *of Kashi, or Cloaked* Demon...'

No one wore cloaks these days. *Except Ashlyn Williams.*

'Mum!' she called, when she opened the front door.

No answer.

'Mum!' She headed through into the kitchen. *Where was her mum?*

She couldn't stop her head churning. Had she really just discovered the killer of Kashi? And... *where was her mum?*

She was starting to panic when she heard a car in the drive. She ran to the front door and opened it to see a black Range Rover pulling up. She realised their own car was missing, just as the passenger door of the huge car opened and her mum climbed out.

'Mum!' Lizzie cried, rushing over to her. 'What's happened?'

'It's OK, Lizzie. I popped into Hebley but the car wouldn't start when I came out of the Spar. Luckily Mr Lennox was there to help.'

'Call me Godwin.'

Lizzie looked round to see the Range Rover's driver standing behind her mum. *That silver hair, distinguished bearing, the riding boots...* With a shock, she realised it was the man from the hunt. He looked at her with a real... *teacher's look.* The sort of teacher who said he had your welfare at heart, when really he was making sure you weren't causing trouble.

'What are we going to do about the car?' Lizzie asked.

Godwin smiled. 'Don't worry about that – I'm getting someone to have a look at it.'

'Thank you again, Godwin,' said Lizzie's mum.

'It's no problem. Anyway, if you're sure you're OK, I'll be off now.'

As he was about to get in the car, he stopped and looked back over his shoulder.

'Are you coming to Eva's party tomorrow?' he asked.

'What?' said Lizzie's mum.

'Eva – Lady Blane's – party. It's her birthday. She always invites newcomers.'

Lizzie tugged her mum's blouse. 'She invited us yesterday, Mum. Remember?'

'I was going to say, if you need a lift I can collect you,' said Godwin.

'I don't know – there's lots of things we have to get done.'

'Oh, go on, Mum…'

Godwin smiled. 'It'll be a good bash,' he said. 'She's very popular. I can introduce you to some of the other villagers.'

'OK, I guess so – and thanks, a lift would be lovely.'

'Great. I'll pick you up at quarter to two.'

As Godwin was reversing the car up the drive Lizzie said: 'Can't we just walk to the party, Mum? It's not far across the fields.'

'What for?'

'I don't like him.'

'You only just met him.'

'No, I saw him when I was out walking. He was *fox hunting*. A pair of women tried to stop him, and he shook his whip at them.'

'I'm sure he didn't do that, Lizzie.'

'He did. I saw it. I thought he was going to hit one of them!'

'Godwin has just done a really kind thing for me – us. He wouldn't do something like that.'

'How do you know?' said Lizzie, turning away. 'You never believe me, do you?' she added, and hurried back into the house.

Her mum shook her head and reached into her bag for her cigarettes. 'Whenever I meet someone nice…' she muttered.

Chapter 6: Lady Blane's Party

Exhausted, Lizzie went to bed early that evening. But she slept poorly, her dreams plagued by images of children being attacked by dark, menacing figures.

In the early morning light she woke panicking, wondering whether Ashlyn had been through the garden that night. Supposing the witch *was* the killer – might she come for Lizzie and her mum in their beds? Should she run and check her mum was OK?

She relaxed as she heard the sound of slippers coming down the landing to the bathroom. But then another frightening thought occurred to her.

Supposing she was the only one who knew the killer's identity?

She had to do something – but what?

*

For once she submitted obediently to her mum's orders to clean the house, as a way of taking her mind off things. After lunch she went upstairs to get ready for Eva's party.

She was pulling on her ankle boots when she heard Godwin's car in the drive.

'Lizzie – our lift's here!' her mum shouted up the stairs.

Pulling a face in the mirror, Lizzie wound her hair up and fastened it into a pony tail. Then she hurried down to join her mum.

As they drove towards Hebley, Lizzie worried what she would do if Ashlyn and Madeline were at the party. She began to fidget, and tried to distract herself by looking at the plush leather interior of the Range Rover and then at Godwin's smooth, confident profile. He was all charm now, chatting to her mum, but she remembered the look on his face when he threatened the saboteurs with his whip. No, she *definitely* didn't like him. And from the repeated, irritating giggles, she was worried her mum was taking a fancy to him. How could she like someone as arrogant – and as old, for that matter – as him? *He wasn't a patch on her dad.*

As they came through the high gates of Eva's manor, Lizzie was instantly captivated by the beautiful manor. Its walls were a hodgepodge of peach brick, bare timber, and whitewashed plaster, criss-crossed by ivy trails. The long, mossy roof sloped down almost to the lawn in places, with large, warped chimney stacks at both ends.

Godwin parked at the end of a line of cars and they got out and went up to a squat, black-timbered door. Godwin rang the bell, and the door was soon opened by Lady Blane.

'How great that you could make it!' said Eva, looking at Lizzie and her mum. 'Come in.'

She hugged them each as they shuffled through the doorway. Lizzie caught the scent of her perfume, which was like fresh lilies.

'Godwin,' Eva said, in a more familiar tone, leaning forward and pecking the tall man on the cheek.

'This way – I'll get you drinks.' Eva led them through into a large sitting room with a roaring fire and dozens of guests standing around, talking loudly and laughing. Winter sunlight streamed through the leaded windows onto the champagne-coloured carpet.

Glancing round, Lizzie recognised several of the villagers. Thomas was near the fireplace, glowering at her whilst his mum chatted to a female vicar with white hair and glasses. The couple who ran the Spar, Mr and Mrs Stykes, were talking to a stocky man and a young, bald Asian-looking man in trendy khakis. She spotted a couple of the other village shopkeepers – but none of the hunt saboteurs.

'How are you settling into your new home?' asked Eva, pouring wine for Godwin and Lizzie's mum.

'It's a bit damp – and full of clutter,' said Lizzie's mum.

'I like it,' said Lizzie. 'There's a library full of all kinds of books, and the garden's amazing.'

Her mum looked at her in surprise. 'You've changed your tune,' she said.

Eva smiled at Lizzie. 'I met your great-uncle a few times,' she said. 'He was wonderful. He loved travelling, and knew a lot about the world and its mysterious ways.'

'I love travelling,' said Lizzie. Again her mum looked at her in disbelief. Lizzie blushed, as vivid images of Kashi's streets flashed in her mind.

The doorbell rang again.

'I'll be back in a mo',' said Eva, and dashed back into the hall.

'She's great, isn't she?' said Godwin, spotting the smile on Lizzie's face. 'Hardly realises how much everyone adores her. And only in the village a couple of years – it normally takes a generation to be accepted in a place like this.'

'Being rich and glamorous probably helps,' said Lizzie's mum. Godwin flushed.

'Two years?' Lizzie repeated. 'I thought she'd been here forever.'

'No. She's European – Eastern European,' said Godwin.

A moment later Eva brought in a young, fresh-faced couple and served them drinks. Lizzie couldn't stop glancing at their hostess. Whilst she wasn't pretty in the way Lizzie usually thought of girls as being pretty, her angular features and dark, swept-back hair made her very striking. She seemed in a different league from the people Lizzie knew.

'Hello again – how's Mr Tubs?'

Lizzie jumped as Mrs Bennett clasped her shoulder. Thomas had sidled up behind his mum.

'He's great,' said Lizzie.

'Good,' said Mrs Bennett briskly. She was a plump woman, with a blushed red face. She craned her neck back to look at the picture on the wall above them. 'I love Eva's taste in art, don't you?' she said.

They all looked up at the painting, which depicted a small, pale-looking fairy with wings, fluttering in a woodland setting.

'Hmm. A bit different from our own feral child…' said Mrs Bennett.

'What?' said Lizzie.

Mrs Bennett glanced bemusedly at her before looking back at the painting. 'Haven't you heard? Hebley has its own Wild Boy of the Woods. If you believe what they say. I'm more inclined to believe in fairies…' She winked at Lizzie.

Lizzie glanced at Thomas who nodded sharply. *Told you so!*

'What do they say?' asked Lizzie.

'There's all kinds of rumours,' said Godwin. 'The Styke's girl, Leanne, from the Spar, saw him first. Night before last. Heard something in the yard, and when she looked out there he was, this little urchin boy rifling through the bins. Then one of my farmers, Burt Eames, came across him in his barn this morning. Said he was wrapped in bin bags, and half-buried in the hay.'

An image of one of the Indian beggar boys flashed in Lizzie's mind.

'… ran off as soon as Burt found him.' Godwin continued, then smiled and added: 'Don't know who was more scared, the boy or Burt!'

Mrs Bennett laughed. 'But if it's true, how will he survive, poor mite?'

'Eating worms and berries,' said Thomas.

'Don't be stupid,' said Lizzie.

'What about the cold?' said her mum. 'He'd get frostbite or hypothermia in this weather, surely?'

'Maybe something terrible's happened to him,' said Mrs Bennett. 'Perhaps he ran away from home or something. Has anyone asked the police if a missing person has been reported?'

'Yes,' said Godwin. He nodded to the stocky man Lizzie had seen, still talking to the trendy young Asian by the fire. 'Jim, the Assistant Chief Constable, has been looking into it. He says there's no record of any boys missing, so there's not much they can do. They can't scour every inch of the countryside, unless there's good reason to. Takes a lot of manpower, that. But he said people should let him know if they see the boy again.'

'I think he's a gypo kid,' said Thomas. 'Escaped from the witches in Hoad's Wood.' He gave Lizzie another fierce stare.

'Thomas! There aren't any witches,' said his mum.

'I wouldn't be so sure,' said Godwin. 'We were riding through there the other day and came across a birch pentagram laid out in a glade – with blood in the centre of it. I think we might know who did that, don't we?' He looked at Lizzie, who began to feel uncomfortable as he showed a flicker of recognition. He *did* remember her from the hunt.

She suddenly got the impression that everyone was looking at her and her mum, as if they were all holding back from saying something. Except for Thomas, who looked as if he was desperate to say it.

'Was my great-uncle one of them?' she asked. Sometimes, she even surprised herself.

Eva's reappearance broke the awkward silence that followed.

'Anyone need more wine?' she asked. The small group broke up, with Godwin offering to sort drinks whilst Mrs Bennett and Lizzie's mum went to sit down. Eva put her arm around Lizzie's shoulder and led her off to one side.

'I'd love to talk with you about your great-uncle,' she said. 'Did you ever meet him?'

'No. Mum says he was a bit of a recluse.'

'He was a famous anthropologist. I'd read lots of his books, but never knew he lived in Hebley until I moved here. It was a shock to realise one of my heroes was living less than a mile away.'

'He was one of your heroes?' said Lizzie, feeling a flicker of pride.

'Yes. I'm passionate about indigenous tribes, and Professor Hartley was a leading authority on several.'

Lizzie's pleasure intensified to hear a member of her family spoken of so respectfully. She'd always considered herself and her family as pretty average. Whilst she'd been proud of her dad, his job as a geologist for a mining company hadn't seemed very exciting.

'Was it true he was a Wiccan?' asked Lizzie. She had to ask someone, and felt she could trust Eva.

The tall woman paused for a moment, as if measuring what she could say. Lizzie waited patiently, used to the slow workings of adults.

'I don't know. Lots of people in the village say he was, and that he got up to some strange things with the others...'

'Others?'

'Yes – there's several witches in the area. Hebley has a reputation for attracting witches and suchlike – druids, spiritualists, mystics – since Victorian times. No one's sure why, but there's plenty of rumours. My advice is to stick clear of them.'

'But wasn't all that stuff about witches being evil just propaganda?' Lizzie asked. 'We learnt it in history. It was just the Church, trying to control women in the Middle Ages.'

'Yes, that's partly true, I can tell you that for sure. But there are good ones and bad ones, and those in the village aren't good. People say they sacrifice animals to their gods.'

'That's terrible,' said Lizzie wrinkling her nose. 'My great-uncle can't have been involved with that!'

'No, I'm sure he wasn't. But I think he might have been lured into their group – by their leader.'

'Who's that?'

'A woman called Ashlyn Williams. Do you know her?'

Lizzie paused for a moment, thinking what to say. 'Yes – I saw her yesterday. She was trying to sabotage a hunt with an older woman. She spoke to me – but she was... strange.'

'Keep away from her, Lizzie,' said Eva sharply. 'She's capable of anything. *Anything*. She lives in Limetree Cottage, just south of the village. The others aren't good to know, either – Madeline Kendall, from the bookshop, and Seth Brown, the woodsman from Godman Hill. Stay away from them all – to be on the safe side.'

'But how could Ashlyn *make* my great-uncle become a witch?'

Eva gave her a significant look. Lizzie blushed, understanding the implication. She remembered what her mum had said about her great-uncle being a ladies' man. *But surely Ashlyn was way too young for him?* Then she thought about her friend Becky's dad, running off with a twenty-two-year-old nurse. *It happened.* Painfully, her thoughts returned to her mum, and what she said about her dad...

'So, what have you been doing since you moved to the country?' asked Eva, changing the subject.

'Cleaning mostly. Mum's *obsessed*. But I've also been exploring the garden.'

'It's a fantastic place, isn't it?' said Eva.

'Yes,' said Lizzie, scrutinising the older woman's eyes, which seemed full of warmth and caring. After a brief pause, Eva said:

'Would you like to come to my stables?'

'Yes please!'

'I could pick you up tomorrow for a ride, if you like. At ten?'

Lizzie beamed.

*

The rest of the afternoon passed very quickly. Eva introduced Lizzie to the Police chief, Jim, who spoke very highly of Godwin, and to the Asian man, Chen Yang, who was an exchange student staying with Eva. Finally she met one of the village's eldest residents, Mr Barrow, who wore a brown suit and tie and knew Evelyn Hartley, her great-uncle's aunt, who was buried in the Rowan Cottage garden.

'She was a strange old bird,' he said, in his broad Herefordshire accent. 'Like her nephew, kept herself to herself.' A glimmer appeared in his rheumy old eyes. 'But she was a *fantastic* gardener. It was her parents who bought the house and started the garden, but she created the magnificent layout you see today. Before she took over the house it was little more than a tangle of brambles and trees.

'I remember Xing, little Xiao Xing, the Chinese kid, who helped her with the work – before her own children mucked in. He must have come off one of the ships at Bristol.' He laughed, and glanced at Lizzie.

'I was a young boy at the time, but we all used to cycle past the gates and shout for *Li'l Xing,* as we called him. He was the first Chinese anyone had ever seen in Hebley.'

For a moment Lizzie had the little Chinese boy in her mind's eye, standing with his fingers between the bars of the gate and watching the flat-capped boys riding past, golden dragons unspooling down his long red coat. *Li'l Xing...*

'... disappeared the following year,' Mr Barrow concluded, giving her a concerned look.

To cover up that she'd lost track of what he was saying, she asked: 'Did Evelyn have lots of visitors?'

'Not many. There was a cocksure little girl with a pony tail, a bit like yours – can't remember her name, though. She was a cheeky little monkey, a relative from the city I think. And then there was that chap Alfred Watkins, who discovered those *ley line* things. He was good friends with Evelyn. What was that club again?

The Woolhope Natural History club. They were into all kinds of strange theories.'

'Ley lines,' Lizzie repeated. She felt sure she'd heard of them.

'Yes – sort of lines of energy underneath the Earth, which you find by dowsing. Watkins said if you looked at a map, you could see churches built in straight lines. He reckoned the builders had been tapping into underground energy, following the ley lines. Ancient routes, used by folk since prehistoric times. The builders didn't know it, of course.'

Lizzie stared at him wide-eyed.

'Poppycock,' he said, emitting another of his sudden loud laughs, and thrusting his big face towards her. 'Don't believe a word of it. I've lived a very, very long time, I'm eighty-seven next month, and I've never experienced anything more than the eye can see. And that's quite enough to keep you going for a lifetime, believe me!'

Shortly after, Lizzie's mum came up and told her that Godwin was going to give them a lift home. Lady Blane came out with them.

'Remember what I said about Ashlyn and her friends,' she told Lizzie, hugging her as she left. 'I'll see you tomorrow.'

Lizzie smiled, thrilled at the thought of the ride.

But driving back through the darkening country lanes, with Godwin and her mum laughing in the front, Lizzie found the afterglow of Eva's party soon slipping away. As much as she tried, she couldn't stop her thoughts returning to the mysterious portal, the murdered girl, and Ashlyn – especially after what Eva had said about her.

What if the witch was the killer? If Lizzie didn't share her suspicions, more children might be killed. She felt her heart sink with the responsibility. She had to talk to someone – someone who could make a difference. But who? Her mum? *Eva?*

After a moment she knew who.

Chapter 7: A Meeting with the Inspector

That night, Lizzie remembered to collect the torch from the kitchen drawer.

Her fear at having to go back through the portal had gradually been replaced by a steely resolve as the evening progressed. *She couldn't be responsible, however indirectly, for another attack.*

Still she found herself struggling to breathe normally as she once again approached the Indian garden.

Everything seemed still and quiet as she came through the first section, but as she approached the Shiva statue her heart leapt as she noticed a sudden movement, at the back beneath the hedge.

She stifled a shriek, at the same time as she saw a dark bushy shape disappear under the yew trees.

A fox – just a fox...

She breathed a sigh of relief, and, muttering to herself to be brave, reached out her hand and began to circle the bronze statue.

As soon as her consciousness returned in the close, dark room, she flicked the torch on and flashed it around.

The beam illuminated damp black walls, smothered in stringy, lime-coloured gunge. Shining the torch down, she spotted a narrow raised ledge going around the wall, which looked like a good way to avoid getting wet feet. She dropped from the alcove on to the ledge, and shone the torch back into the hole. Carved into the back of the rock was a portrait of a creature with four primitive-looking heads, each glaring in different directions. Beside the creature squatted a fat bird, like a hen. She guessed they were probably Hindu gods, but had no idea which ones.

In a corner of the room she found a waist-high, rectangular structure assembled from stone blocks. The structure was hollow like a well, so she looked around for something to drop into it and test its depth. Flashing the torch about, she noticed what appeared to be a piece of white rock sticking out of the water. She crunched over to it and lifted it up.

As soon as the torch lit the shadowy eye sockets and tapered, yellow teeth she dropped the object, realising what it was – a human skull! She realised what she'd been walking on each time she wobbled and splashed her way through the chamber – *skeletons.*

There were bones everywhere, mostly submerged in the shallow water except for the odd jutting femur, or clawing ribcage. *How did they all get here?* For an instant Lizzie's head swam with confusion and alarm, imagining she was in the gruesome den of the child killer. But then she forced herself to think rationally. *No one could have killed that many people, surely?* She had no idea how long the bones had been here. In one of her great-uncle's books she'd read about a thing called an ossuary, where monks kept the bones of dead holy men. Maybe this was one of those. Still, she didn't fancy picking anything else up to test the well, so she removed her warm clothing, stashed it at the bottom of the stairs, and, with a final shudder, headed up into the open air.

Outside, the sky was overcast and a grey haze had permeated the ghats, dulling the yellows and browns of the buildings. The air was humid and stifling, and Lizzie was soon sweating heavily as she puffed up the steps into the city.

She spoke first to a young man, who tossed his head dismissively to indicate he didn't understand her, and then to an older man with bottle-bottom glasses who was not only able but enthusiastic to give her directions to the police station.

The station was a pale blue concrete building ten minutes' walk from the river, set back from one of the busy main roads. A sign above the entrance contained the neat spider-leg scrawl of Hindi, with the word 'POLICE' painted in green below it. A stiff-backed guard with a handlebar moustache and a rifle eyed Lizzie suspiciously as she sidled through the open doors.

The main hall of the station was divided down the middle by a high counter with a glass panel, behind which police men and women dealt patiently with the urgent pleas of wronged citizens. The public area overflowed with people, either jostling for position at the counter, in heated discussions with one another, or sitting fatalistically on the floor, waving off flies.

Lizzie faltered, overwhelmed by the chaos. How would she get past everyone? *What if he wasn't here?*

Then, in a stroke of luck, the young Inspector Faruwallah emerged from a side corridor with an old woman leaning on his arm. He glanced up and immediately spotted Lizzie, the only white person in the room. Saying a few quiet words to the woman, and then barking angrily at a poor-looking man who started to tug his arm, the Inspector came over to her.

'I know you,' he said. 'You ran away from me, didn't you? After the murder.'

Lizzie nodded. 'Yes. But I'm not going to run away this time,' she said humbly. 'I need to talk to you.'

A well-built boy with short-cropped black hair and a heavy jaw sprang over to them, saying: 'You England? England girl? Yes?' He looked at Raj. 'Is England girl, Mr Police…'

The Inspector said something to him in Hindi and waved him away with his hand.

'What's your name, England girl?' asked the boy, reaching out for Lizzie's shoulder.

Again Raj shouted, and the boy backed off, but didn't stop gawping.

'Come to my office,' said Raj, in his refined accent. 'I think we need some privacy.'

Lizzie followed him down the corridor past several doors inset with windows, through which she could see officers and clerks typing at computers. Many of the rooms had no external windows, being lit only by stark neon lights. She felt reassured to see a high number of women officers.

The Inspector's office was up a flight of concrete stairs at the back of the building. It was a small room, with an over-sized fan turning feebly on the ceiling, and a window looking out across an empty courtyard.

'Please, have a seat,' said Raj. He beckoned her to a wooden chair as he sat down behind his desk. 'Would you like some water? It's treated.' Lizzie gratefully took the glass he poured, and quickly glugged it down.

'Now, tell me who you are, and where you come from,' said Raj, leaning forward and looking at her intently.

'My name's Lizzie Jones. I come from England – London originally, but now I live in Herefordshire.'

'Ah, a lovely county!' Raj exclaimed. 'So beautiful and green.'

'You've been there?' asked Lizzie, surprised.

'Yes. I studied in England,' he said, with a self-satisfied smokiness in his eyes. 'The Police college I went to in Mumbai – which you probably know as Bombay – had an exchange with one of your training colleges near Warwick. I spent six months there with the Serious Crimes Unit. It was a busy period, but I managed to get out once or twice. I visited Hereford, where I had an uncle. Poor Uncle Mehul, he was practically the only Indian in the city! But it was a lovely place; the cathedral was glorious. I also went to Ludlow, which was very charming. I particularly liked all the timber-framed buildings. Have you been there?'

'No,' said Lizzie, wondering if he might talk all day. Before he had time to continue, she added: 'I like your city too.' She thought again how big and chaotic and beautiful Kashi was, especially at the ghats. She'd never imagined anything like it.

'Thank you,' said the Inspector. 'Now tell me – why did you run off the other day?' Sensing her apprehension, he added: 'You can trust me completely.'

'I don't know,' said Lizzie. 'I was so upset to see that girl, what someone had done to her. How could anyone do that? I'm sorry I ran. I was frightened, and wanted to get back to my parents…'

Raj nodded, as if that was reasonable enough. 'Do you know anything about the crime?' he asked.

'I'm not sure. But when I got back to my parents, I thought about something you said, about a *pee-*something was it? Wearing a cloak or something? I think I might've seen someone wearing a cloak….'

'Pisaca,' said Raj. 'In Hinduism, a Pisaca is a demon who eats humans, and that is what people have been calling the child killer. There are legends of the Pisaca and her followers going back a long time. We have recently had one of our most precious artefacts stolen, a holy Lingam of Shiva, and people think that without its sacred protection the demon has returned, to resume preying on the blood of innocents.

'And yes, to answer your question, there have been reports of someone around the scenes of the murders wearing a cloak – but not all of the time. The reports are not consistent, and I believe some are the result of hysteria – people conjuring up in their minds things they have heard others talking about. Some say the killer is a woman, pale and haunting like a ghost, but others say the creature they have seen is more corporeal but terrifying, with horrible teeth and yellow eyes like a cat or a goat. And then there are others who swear that the killer is a manifestation of Kali herself.'

'Of who?'

'Kali – the demonic incarnation of one of our goddesses, Parvati, Lord Shiva's wife. They used to sacrifice children and animals to Kali in the past. As one of the sightings happened near the Kali temple people have been saying that the toothless old crone is back, because it's been too long since she had a proper blood sacrifice.'

Lizzie's eyes widened.

'It's all piffle, of course,' he added. 'Superstitious nonsense.'

'Do you believe in Kali?'

The Inspector scratched his plump cheek. 'I consider myself a Hindu,' he said. 'But I believe our gods and goddesses – of which we have a lot, over a million some say – are just human symbols for a unity that is ultimately unknowable. They are representations to help give us a handle on the great mystery of our

111

universe. I don't admire the literalism of those who believe these gods are real. They are people with no imagination. Backward folk, country folk.'

Lizzie nodded. Much of what the Inspector was saying was passing her by, but she liked his relaxed air of knowledge and confidence. He sounded highly reasonable, as if he must be telling the truth. And she agreed with his idea about the mystery of the universe: whenever she thought about the origins of the world she always felt small and insignificant, but still in awe of it all.

'Where is the Kali temple?' she asked.

'It's in the Old Town, near the Marble Palace.'

Lizzie nodded thoughtfully.

'So, young lady,' said Raj. 'Tell me what you have seen. Our city is panicking, scared for the lives of its children. People want nothing more than to see this killer – or these killers – caught!'

Lizzie had prepared her story. 'I saw a woman in a cloak, a couple of days' ago. But not at the fountain where that girl was murdered – it was down near the ghats.'

'Good,' said Raj. 'What did she look like?'

'She was quite tall, with long, frizzy, sort of reddish hair, and green eyes. And she had pale skin – she was English, you could tell. She was probably... maybe...

twenty-five…perhaps?' Lizzie was terrible with ages, at least of adults, but she scrutinised the Inspector's face for any sign of recognition. She was pleased to see him nodding, writing it down on a note pad with a pencil. 'Does that sound like what the others said?'

'Yes,' said Raj thoughtfully. 'It does. We had one witness who said she was a redhead. A reliable witness, a woman lawyer in the Old Town. And even the green eyes fit with that description. But then we've had someone else swear she had dark hair, too. And a tailor in Massi Street even told me she had wings, and flew off into the night when he saw her! But I think we can safely dismiss that one. Where was she, and what was she doing when you saw her?'

'She was walking down the ghat near Dash-ash – Dashashwim…'

'Dashashwamedha ghat?'

'Yes, that's it. She was walking along there, with her head down. She looked serious, like she was thinking deeply about something.' Lizzie recalled the expression on Ashlyn's face when she'd come through the gap in the hedge.

'Which way was she heading?'

'Up into the city, up the ghats. I didn't see where she went, though.'

'OK. What time was it when you saw her?' asked Raj, scribbling furiously.

'Early in the morning, just after dawn. Me and my family were out on a boat ride on the river.' As she spoke Lizzie noticed two framed photographs on the wall. One was a panorama of a grand European-style city, and the other was of a short, fat Indian couple. The couple were looking proudly at the camera, and she wondered if they were the Inspector's parents.

'Good,' said Raj. 'This is very helpful. I will file a report for our records, and have an officer talk to the people who work round there. Is there anything else?'

'No, I don't think so.'

'OK. Well, thank you for coming in. I know it takes a lot of courage to do these things, particularly in a strange place. Whereabouts are you staying with your parents? It will help me if I know where I can get hold of you if I need to.'

'We're at Hotel Rama,' said Lizzie. She'd spotted the hotel when exploring the far end of town near the cremation ghat.

'Rama,' said Raj, scrawling it down on the pad. 'That's great. Now, if there's nothing else, I'll see you out.'

When he'd shown her to the front steps of the station he said: 'Thank you again for your help, Miss

Jones. As I said before, you shouldn't be walking round the city on your own. Do you want me to get you an escort back to your hotel?'

'No, I'll be all right, honestly.'

'OK. But promise me you'll go straight back to your parents, and stick to the main roads. No side alleys!'

'Yes, I will,' said Lizzie.

*

The Inspector watched the girl as she dodged between the traffic and disappeared down a lane on the opposite side of the road. Then he pulled out his mobile and selected a number.

'Hi, it's me,' he said, in Hindi. 'The English girl is back. Yes... She says she saw the white woman on Dashashwamedha... The one the lawyer saw, yes, the redhead... I told her about the Kali rumour... She asked where the temple was... Yes, yes. I have a hunch she might go there too. Are you still filming at the palace?... Yes. You can check on her?... Good. Do you think she'll recognise you?... On Ramses! That'll give her a surprise...'

The Inspector finished his call, smiled and shook his head, then turned back into the building.

Chapter 8: Ramses IV

The temple of Kali was located in a warren of back streets beneath the giant whitewashed walls of the Marble Palace.

The temple had seen better days. Its cupolas were pitted and crumbling away. The painted frescoes depicting scenes of the demon goddess spearing, gutting, and tearing the heads off her enemies had all but faded, leaving behind pocked, bare stone. Flagstones in the outer sanctum had cracked, and pools of water had formed from the rain which found its way in through holes in the roof. Sitting about on the temple's sikhara was a tribe of large monkeys, with light brown fur and long, pink faces. Their tails hung over the temple eaves, flicking insolently as they dropped husks of stolen fruit into the paths of passersby.

But, despite its appearance, the temple was not derelict. At the heart of the structure, in the inner sanctum – a dark, undecorated cell containing a stone image of the six-armed deity with her necklace of skulls

– a woman was at worship, offering up sweet cakes and rice to the goddess. She placed the food in a bowl at the foot of the effigy.

From a vantage point on a narrow flight of steps between two houses, Lizzie watched as the woman emerged from the sanctum after performing her worship. The woman was wearing scarlet robes, with the orange neck cord which Lizzie now knew represented the brahmin, or priest, caste. She was quite young – perhaps in her early twenties – with short-cropped black hair, and an appealingly round face.

After leaving Inspector Faruwallah, Lizzie had asked around for directions to the temple. She sensed trepidation in the first few people she asked, but eventually an elderly gentleman had told her that it was on the way to his cousin's rug shop, and led her here. As they walked the man explained that the great palace looming over this part of town was owned by Sabadhassi, a fabulously wealthy industrialist who was very popular and liked the movies. In fact Sabi – as he was affectionately known – loved Bollywood so much he was currently letting a film company use his palace for the making of a new epic, starring someone very famous whose name sounded something like *Roshnagra*. At the top of the steps the man had suggested she come to have a look at his cousin's rugs, but she thanked him politely and declined.

Now, as she watched, a man in white robes with a turban came hurrying down the road and stopped at the entrance to the temple. Before going in, he glanced around and Lizzie recognised him at once as the priest from the riverfront, Hanu. She looked down as his eyes swept across her, certain he would see her. She prepared to run.

But when she looked up Hanu was disappearing inside the temple. She saw the young priestess greet him, then they went into the inner sanctum.

Bolstered by her success with Raj, Lizzie had intended to spy on the temple for a while, on the off-chance Ashlyn might go there. But seeing Hanu made her feel unsafe. *Had he seen her?* She didn't know, but decided it was best to head back to the portal anyway.

To return to the waterfront, she had to skirt around the back of the temple and work her way up through the network of passages and alleyways beneath the Marble Palace. Despite Raj's warning, she didn't know any other way to go. But, as she hurried through the narrow, shaded streets, she soon began to feel a sense of uneasiness.

What was Hanu doing all the way over here? She remembered their encounter on the ghat. There was something about the way he grabbed her wrist, and the intensity of his look, which had frightened her. But it was more than that. As he'd stared into her eyes, there'd been real scrutiny there, almost as if he knew her – or knew of her. She'd distanced herself from it at the time but now, thinking back, it was clear.

Despite the closeness of the heat she shuddered, and quickened her pace.

Soon she noticed something else strange – there was no one around. In England that wouldn't have been so surprising but here, even down the back streets, there was always someone milling about, or leaning out of a window watching the world go by. But for the last few minutes she'd been walking through deserted alleys, and an increasingly eerie silence. *Something didn't feel right.*

She came out into a slightly wider street with the steep palace wall on one side and a concrete building which appeared to be a warehouse on the other. The height of the two structures blocked out much of the daylight, keeping the street in perpetual gloom. At the foot of the warehouse wall she had to step around a heap of black and rotting vegetables, mostly cabbages and carrots. She covered her nose with her sleeve to keep out the rancid, vinegary smell.

Then, as she followed the alley along the gentle curve of the palace wall, she noticed a faint sound coming from up ahead. The noise, like a nail scraping slowly down a blackboard, seemed to originate from a small, dingy-looking passage. The sound was so faint she wouldn't have noticed it in another part of the city.

It came again, except this time louder, as if whoever – or whatever – was making it was coming down the passageway towards her. She wondered if it might be an animal, perhaps one of those sacred cows, catching the wall with its big horns. Or maybe it was a man pushing a rickety old cart? She glanced back over her shoulder, hoping someone else might have appeared. But the street was empty.

And then she heard the sound again, but this time coming from where the alley curved away *behind* her. She began to feel nervous.

At that moment, something happened to the atmosphere around her. The temperature dropped, and the air itself seemed to somehow quiver and brush against her skin. She shook her head, as the light in the alleyway became at once silvery yet dim, like a film in negative. Suddenly she had an overwhelming desire *not* to know what it was that was making the noise, and she looked around for a means of escape from the alley. But there were no nearby doors or passages, and above her only the towering, featureless walls of the palace and warehouse, with a strip of grey sky between them.

And then the women emerged. Or at least Lizzie assumed they were women, but at the same time she couldn't help noticing that there seemed to be something very different about them. Something strange, not quite *human*.

There were three of them, two ahead, and one coming up the alleyway behind her. Their skin was scabrous and surprisingly dark, in a way that seemed to absorb and deaden light. Their yellowish eyes had a focused, calculating look, like cobras advancing towards prey. At first Lizzie thought the strangest thing about them was their nakedness, but then, as they started taking slow, arching steps towards her, she realised that even weirder were their small, sharp teeth, glistening grey between their wet lips. With the way each tapered towards a fine point, the teeth looked as if they'd been *filed*.

'What do you want?' Lizzie shouted, but the women didn't reply. They just kept advancing towards her, their mouths opening wider to reveal thick, plum-coloured tongues. The one behind began to emit short, steam-like hisses.

Lizzie was seized by panic. She didn't know how it happened but in the next moment she was scrambling up the palace wall, her fingers and toes managing to find the tiniest chips and indents in the stone. She stretched for even smaller holds above her, heading for one of the high windows. The creatures – *surely not normal women?* – ran for her, and, as one leapt agilely up the wall Lizzie noticed how long her fingernails were, like talons, before she instinctively coiled up to avoid the strike. She lost her grip and began to fall backwards, but instead of going straight down she managed to push away from the wall so she was able to leap over the women and land on the other side of the alley.

The women spun to face her, coming together as if one creature, the three heads, six arms, and six legs all moving with surprising co-ordination. They transfixed Lizzie with hungry eyes and started to advance. She backed away and soon felt the firmness of the warehouse behind her.

She glanced around fearfully, wondering what to do. There were no doors or alleys nearby, she knew that. Groping behind her, she felt the smoothness of the concrete and realised there was little hope of climbing the wall. Then, in the middle of the alleyway ahead, she noticed an open manhole cover. *Maybe she could get to that and escape down the sewers?* It was a desperate idea, but better than letting those teeth and claws get any closer.

But before she even took a step towards the manhole one of the black-skinned women seemed to read her mind, and darted sideways to stand in front of it. The other two continued to advance towards her. Spreading their arms wide, they began to rock their hips and flex their taloned fingers, as if getting ready to seize her.

What do they want? Lizzie thought wildly.

Now she could clearly see their cold, yellow eyes, boring into her as if to drain her will. She felt herself weakening, and wondered what would happen if she just gave in and allowed the women to do what they would with her. As her last hope she took a deep breath, preparing to put all her energy into one final scream.

Then, just as the front two were reaching forward to grab her, a mighty blaring noise filled the air.

Lizzie and the women froze, looking down towards the far end of the alley where the sound had come from. It came again, like a chair being scraped across a floor, and then the maker of the noise came into sight.

It was a huge, caparisoned elephant, its head and ears painted garishly with blue-and-yellow flowers, gold-fringed crimson cloth draped over its crown and down its sides. Sat on its back was a boy dressed in a resplendent white tunic and red turban.

As soon as the boy saw Lizzie and the women he shouted and the elephant began to trot down the alley towards them. Feeling strangely detached, Lizzie watched the great creature in awe. She marvelled at how its brightly-painted ears bounced lightly against its head, and how its massive body nearly filled the passageway. For a moment, she wondered if this was how she was going to die, crushed by a stampeding elephant…

The creatures with the sharp teeth turned their attention to the beast too, hissing even more and showing their lurid tongues as if to try and frighten it away. But Lizzie noticed they were moving closer together again, like a nest of snakes protecting themselves.

Just before they reached the manhole cover, the boy shouted and the elephant stopped. There was a moment's silence, and then the great beast began to emit an ultra-low, rumbling sound, which Lizzie could feel coming up through the ground. The elephant lowered its head and tusks but kept its eyes fixed on the women, full of raw, Lord-of-the-Jungle threat.

The women shared a quick glance and then, with a few sharp sounds like hot metal thrust into cold water, they began to walk backwards slowly down the alley, as if to make it clear that, whilst beaten, they hadn't lost face. The elephant continued to emit the rumbling sound until they had disappeared from sight.

At that moment Lizzie looked up at the boy. There was something about his smiling face that looked familiar…

'Let me introduce you to the Great Pharaoh, Ramses the Fourth,' he said, swinging out of the saddle and slipping down the caparison to land triumphantly on his feet before her.

'You're – *you*!' Lizzie exclaimed. 'The boy from the marketplace!'

'I'm flattered you remember my name,' he said, but his expression remained relaxed and she sensed he was only teasing. 'Pandu,' he added.

'Pandu,' she repeated, then cried: 'You stole my watch!' It was the first thing that came into her head.

Pandu snorted. 'I save your life from those - *people*, whoever they are – and all you can do is accuse me of petty theft!'

Lizzie frowned. She felt woozy, still in shock. 'Well – did you?'

'What?'

'Steal my watch?'

'Yes.' He moved over to where the women had been standing, and peered at the dirt.

Realising the boy felt no remorse, Lizzie decided there was no point in pursuing the accusations further.

'*What were they?*' she said in a suddenly shrill voice, as the tension of the encounter flooded back.

Pandu rubbed at the sand on the street. 'Naked women with *very* long toenails,' he said. 'Look at these footprints.'

Lizzie stood by him and looked down. It was true, most of them were scuffed but in places she could see the long gashes of their nails – more like claws than toenails.

'They had sharp teeth,' she said nervously, biting her thumbnail. 'Did you see how black their skin was?'

'Probably Dravidians,' said Pandu. 'From the South. Tamil Nadu or somewhere.'

'Drav-what-y-uns?'

'Dravidians,' Pandu repeated. 'They're the non-Aryan Indians, from the south. They have much blacker skin, they're an older ethnic group than we northerners. They were probably from some godforsaken village in the middle of nowhere. I bet they have something to do with the Kali cult.'

'Their skins weren't just black,' said Lizzie, incredulously. 'They were *black*. Like coal. Did you see? They didn't look like real *people*.'

Pandu stood up straight. 'Mmm,' he said, thinking. Suddenly he said: 'Do you want a ride on an elephant?

I need to get back to set, and I don't think you should be hanging round here on your own.'

Lizzie thought wildly for a moment. *She should go home.* She'd only meant to tell the Inspector about Ashlyn, then go back. She wondered what time it was, but realised she had no way of knowing. *Because he nicked my watch,* she thought, looking at the boy's bare wrist. *Had he sold it?*

'OK,' she said. She couldn't stand the thought of being alone again.

They walked back to the elephant, which was still standing motionless, blocking the alleyway. As Lizzie approached, it lifted its trunk steadily towards her. She noticed the fleshy nub at the end, curling over and around on itself as it hovered near her chin. She glanced at Pandu.

'He's just checking you out,' he said. 'Aren't you, Rammy?'

'He looks sad,' Lizzie said, tentatively touching the trunk. The pinkish-grey flesh felt dry, like cardboard. 'Why have you painted him all those stupid colours?' She didn't approve of dressing animals up, they weren't playthings.

'You ask a lot of questions, don't you?' said Pandu. 'You'll soon see.'

He showed her how to climb on to the elephant with the use of the saddling straps. In the middle of the creature's back was a piece of padded white cotton sewn in between the two sections of red velvet that hung down its flanks. Lizzie sat on this, behind Pandu. At first it was slightly uncomfortable, she could feel the creature's spine digging into her buttocks, but then it dawned on her that she was sitting on top of a *real live elephant* and before she knew it her thoughts were distracted from the strange women. Below, the street was a thrillingly long way down, and, at eye level, she could see into the windows of the warehouse, where giant metal hooks hung from rafters.

'We'll need to go round the streets in a circle,' explained Pandu. 'Can't turn around or reverse, you see. Hold on to my back.'

At a command from the boy, Ramses IV started walking forward. Lizzie cautiously placed her hands under Pandu's arms, feeling his skinny ribs. Initially she was tense, worrying she might fall off, but soon she relaxed, and felt her hips and shoulders shifting up and down, back and forth with the gentle movement of the beast. Her grip on Pandu lightened and, as they headed down the deserted alleyway, she began to grin. Then she asked Pandu the next big question on her mind:

'How come you turned up at just the right moment?'

Pandu kept looking forward, barking the odd command at the elephant as he spoke.

'I told you I work at the temple of Ganesh, where I look after Ramses,' he said. 'But I do other things too. At the moment I'm helping the police with their investigations into the murders. You know Inspector Faruwallah – Raj? I'm helping him. We've been looking for clues about the Pisaca. I've been spending some time hanging around the places she's been seen, looking for anything suspicious. For strange-looking foreigners.' He leaned back and gave her a wink.

'You're helping *the police?*'

'Yes,' replied Pandu, without further explanation. Lizzie thought something like that, a child helping to do detective work, would never happen back home. She wished it would.

'Have you been round the ghats?' she asked.

'Yes. Mainly Dashashwamedha.'

'Is that where you saw me?'

'Yes. You have good powers of deduction, you'd make a good detective yourself.' Lizzie couldn't tell if he was being sarcastic – but assumed he was.

'I followed you after you left the Kali priest, Hanu,' he continued. 'But when I finally got the opportunity to speak to you, you weren't so easy to talk to.'

'But how come you're here now?'

'Raj called me after you'd been to see him at the station. He told me you'd seen someone matching the description of the Pisaca, and that he'd told you about the suspected connection with the Kali temple. He thought you might come down here, and I said I'd check on you. I'm working just up there,' he said gesturing at the palace, 'and it was lunch break so I agreed. But I was coming down by another route altogether. You've got Ramses to thank for the change of direction. He suddenly stopped and refused to go on. Eventually, I let him go his way, and that's how we found you here with your friends.'

'The *elephant* knew where I was?'

'He's got sensitive feet,' said Pandu, matter-of-factly. 'Elephants can detect things for miles through the ground. It was probably *them* he sensed.'

Lizzie felt a sudden intense affection for the beast. *Who knew what those women might have done to her, if it hadn't been for him?*

'Do you think they might be connected with the murders?' she asked.

'I haven't heard anything about them before. But it's certainly possible. I don't think they wanted to stop you for a chat,' he said, grinning. Then he added: 'There's a theory there's more than one person involved in the killings. We'll report it back to Raj. But not just now, I've got some other work to do, and I'm already late.'

They had circled back into the populated streets, and people, scooters, and rickshaws were parting silently as if it was entirely natural for an elephant to be coming at them down the centre of the road.

Looking down Ramses' flank, Lizzie watched a couple of small children in scruffy, embroidered outfits entertaining a party of European tourists who'd spilled out of a coach for tea and cigarettes. The boy was patting a bongo drum and the girl was shaking a tambourine and singing in a high, beautiful voice. But as Lizzie and Pandu came by on Ramses the tourists turned away from the little entertainers to photograph the decorated elephant. Lizzie saw the pinched anger on the boy's face.

'Why do you think there might be more than one person doing the killings?' asked Lizzie.

'Cha!' shouted Pandu at the elephant, then repeated urgently, 'Cha! Cha! Ramses...' One of the tourists had tossed some money out of the coach window at the two children, causing them to stop performing and chase the rolling coins into the road. The elephant lurched to a halt as the little girl jumped desperately in between its giant feet.

'Careless bloody tourists!' Pandu shouted at the man on the coach, who had a long, passive looking face and large glasses. The man shrunk back into his seat. From feeling like a princess, Lizzie felt suddenly ashamed of her nationality.

Once the girl was clear from between the elephant's legs, Pandu urged Ramses off again.

'I believe the killings are linked to the Kali cult,' he said, as if there hadn't been an interruption. 'Raj told you who Kali is?'

'Sure. She's the wife of Shiva. In her demonic form,' said Lizzie, remembering carefully what Raj had told her.

'That's right. Throughout history, Kali has been associated with the most barbaric acts in the name of religion. Have you ever heard of the Thugees?'

'No.'

'They were a band of Kali worshippers – *Kapilikas* – who used to join up with travellers on the road and gain their friendship and trust. Then, in the middle of the night, they would sneak up on them, and garrotte them with cords. It's where your word *thug* comes from.'

'Why did they do that?'

'Because it honoured the goddess.'

Lizzie screwed up her face in disbelief.

'There were many other forms of torture and killing associated with Kali,' Pandu continued. 'Much of it done as a form of sacrifice. Most often the victims were goats and other animals, but in Calcutta they used to behead a boy every week. The city even got its name from the goddess.'

'So you think these recent child killings might be a form of sacrifice to Kali? And that there might be several worshippers doing the sacrifices?' Lizzie remembered what Lady Blane had said about the Hebley witches, making animal sacrifices to their gods.

'Yes, it's possible. Some people have even suggested that the Pisaca is a manifestation of Kali herself. People have become too complacent, too obsessed with money, they say. The goddess of darkness and destruction feels it's time to shake everything up, to make people focus on the true path of the spirit once more.'

'You mean they're killing people to make others more *spiritual*?' said Lizzie. That didn't make any sense.

Pandu looked round at her. He didn't say anything, but his expression was devoid of its usual humour.

'You don't believe that, do you?'

'I don't believe it's right. But I know these people, and it's easy to imagine they could think that way,' he said.

'Well, I don't believe it! Spirituality's a good thing. It's – it's the opposite of killing kids!'

Pandu shrugged. She noticed that he looked particularly miserable all of a sudden, staring down at the back of the elephant's head.

'Pandu, why have you become so involved in the investigations?' she asked, after a few moments' silence.

As the boy glanced at her over his shoulder, she noticed again how deep and dark his eyes were, like rich, polished wood.

'Because they took my brother.'

At that moment Ramses drew to a halt. They had reached the gates of the palace.

Chapter 9:   The Rose of Kashi

On sight of the painted elephant, the two Sikhs guarding the Marble Palace turned and began to push the large wooden gates open.

'We're going in *there*?' asked Lizzie, all thoughts of going home instantly vanishing.

'Yes,' said Pandu, easing Ramses forward through the archway. The two children ducked their heads as they went through.

They emerged into a giant courtyard, with the ornate, turreted palace before them and several small shrines and outhouses to either side. A few large trees provided a splash of greenery against the buildings' blazing white.

But more awesome than the palace itself was the frantic activity taking place in its courtyard. There must have been over a hundred people bustling about, with many of them clustered around large items of black equipment which Lizzie quickly realised were lights, cameras and microphones. On one side of the courtyard, in the shade of a giant tree, three more decorated elephants shuffled around, their riders kitted out like Pandu in white tops and scarlet turbans. Across from them, a group of neatly-groomed people in red and yellow outfits stood in a rectangle before a shrine draped with purple curtains. Everyone everywhere seemed to be yelling, like a ship's crew in a storm.

'A film set!' Lizzie exclaimed.

'Yes. The film's called *The Rose of Kashi*,' said Pandu, smiling and hoisting himself around in the saddle to face the rectangle of people.

A fat man on a high chair near the cameras bellowed and everyone went quiet. A moment later an upbeat Hindi duet between a man and woman began blaring from a giant amp, and the people in front of the shrine began to dance energetically.

To Lizzie, the dance was one of the most passionate and exciting things she'd ever seen. The men wore long, fanning red gowns over baggy white leggings, and the women had bright lemon saris which flared and collapsed like sails as they twirled and quick-stepped about. Everything was done at such a pace, with seemingly impossible elegance and poise. As she watched, Lizzie longed to be a dancer too.

At the centre of the group were a man with a bouffant haircut and an exceptionally beautiful, slight woman with a long black pony tail. These were evidently the leads, and every so often the group would break up to allow them to spring and pirouette together. It was only towards the end that Lizzie realised they were miming the words of the song to each other, for the benefit of the zoomed-in cameras.

The dance finished with two dozen flushed faces smiling at the camera, all arms and legs stretching away from the central, kneeling couple. Lizzie had to stop herself from clapping.

Then the man on the high chair shouted in Hindi, the dancers broke apart, and the crowd began once more to mill about.

Lizzie noticed Pandu had resumed his customary grin. 'What do you reckon?' he asked.

'Brilliant!' she exclaimed. 'What's it about?'

'It's the story of the love between a rural boy and an urban twenty-first century girl,' said Pandu. 'The boy's played by Romesh Nagra, and the girl by Vona Makkouk. You've heard of them, I suppose?'

Lizzie shook her head.

'You've never heard of Vona Makkouk?'

Lizzie raised her eyebrows. 'Should I?'

'Of course! She's one of India's most famous actresses. She's always in London and New York with your celebrities. She was going out with Ryan Gosling only last year. You've heard of *him*, I assume?'

Lizzie didn't bother answering. Pandu began edging Ramses through the crowd, over towards the other elephants. 'I'm needed for the next scene,' he said.

Lizzie kept watching the lead actors as the set hands brought them water bottles and towels to mop their faces. Two older teenagers followed them about with large black umbrellas to shelter them from the sun, which was starting to break through the clouds. Lizzie thought the man, Romesh, looked a bit silly, too old and overweight to play a romantic lead. *Paunchy*, that's the word her dad would have used for him. He looked like he'd do a good Elvis impersonation. But she did think the young actress, Vona Makkouk, was stunning, with a real air of glamour about her. All eyes followed her as she moved about and effortlessly charmed members of the crowd.

'Now, this man you *will* know,' said Pandu, as they approached the tree where the other elephants stood fidgeting in the humid air.

Sitting on a folding chair in the shade of the tree was a middle-aged, stocky man with patchy stubble and a partially unwound turban. He had heavy-lidded eyes and broad lips, and was swigging from a silver hip flask.

The man shook his head and grinned as the children approached on Ramses.

'Pandu! Where have you been, you young roister?' he bellowed. 'Off chasing skirt, by the look of things!'

Lizzie felt her cheeks burn, and sweat prickle in her hair. *How could he say something like that?* She realised the man's tan was fake – in places it seemed to have worn away entirely, either rubbed off or washed away by sweat. She guessed he wasn't really Indian.

'Mister Richard Pike – may I introduce... um, Lizzie,' said Pandu, with mock formality.

Dick Pike! Lizzie *had* heard of him. He was a has-been actor who'd starred in a lot of horror films a few years ago. Lizzie used to persuade her mum to let her stay up late to watch them, but always used to fall asleep before the end. Dick Pike would usually play the wolfman, vampire, or evil aristocrat. But she hadn't heard anything about him for a long time, and had thought he was dead.

'Pleased to meet you, young lady,' said the old actor, inclining his head and saluting her with the flask. Lizzie wondered what was in it.

'Dick plays an eccentric lawyer, Gafur Mahmood,' said Pandu. 'He's trying to find Romesh, to let him know he's inherited a small fortune from a long-lost uncle.'

'Load of bloody tosh!' said Dick, guffawing. He looked round and saw a young Hindu man in a sky-blue short-sleeve shirt approaching.

'You elephant guys ready now?' asked the man, squinting up at them. 'You're on for the next scene.'

Lizzie had to climb down from Ramses, and Pandu suggested that she wait in a sheltered corridor nearby, where she could watch the shoot.

In the scene, an evidently inebriated Dick Pike was fleeing from a band of thieves who were after the leather briefcase clutched beneath his arm. When the director called for action, Dick came pelting out into an artificially constructed square – Lizzie couldn't believe she hadn't noticed a whole fake façade of buildings erected in the courtyard – and ran straight into the four elephants and their riders. One of the elephants had an ornately-carved box strapped to its back, with a light canvas awning. Sitting on a pile of cushions in the box was a handsomely dressed boy with a golden turban and dreamy expression. As soon as Dick and the muggers appeared, a comic scene ensued involving an elaborate chase around the stumbling legs of the elephants. The richly dressed youth lurched exaggeratedly from side-to-side, as his elephant tried to avoid stamping on Dick. Lizzie was impressed at how well the old actor managed to dodge and dive about in the dangerous stunt, especially considering how drunk he seemed.

'He only got into the film because he's Sabi's son.'

Lizzie, thoroughly engrossed, twisted round to see who'd spoken to her. It was the lead actress, Vona Makkouk.

Lizzie had thought Vona looked glamorous from a distance, but up close she seemed even more perfect. Her skin was unblemished and radiant, the colour of coffee in sunlight. Her bronze lips parted in a broad smile to reveal dazzling white teeth with a cute little gap in the middle. But above all it was her glowing brown eyes which were most gorgeous, like windows on a soul polished by all the best experiences in life.

'I'm Vona Makkouk,' she said, holding out her petite hand for Lizzie to shake.

'Hello,' said Lizzie. 'I'm Lizzie – Lizzie Jones.'

'I haven't seen you round before. Are you cast or crew? Or don't tell me – family?'

'Um – I'm just here with a friend.'

'Who's that?'

'Pandu?' There was no sign of recognition. 'He's one of the elephant riders?'

Lizzie noticed Vona pull a quick face before carrying on. 'I thought you might be related to Dick. You *are* English?'

'Yes.'

'I stayed in London for six months a couple of years ago. We were filming *Cry Baby, Cry*. It was such a laugh. I so love England.'

They looked back at the scene in progress. Sabi's son had had his turban knocked off against the side of the carriage, and his long hair was falling down across his face.

Vona rolled her eyes. 'He couldn't act to save his life,' she said.

'Is he really Sabi's son?' asked Lizzie.

'Oh yes. His dad thinks he's wonderful. It was a deal done with Bobesh, the director, for the use of the palace grounds. That and quite a few *crore* of rupees, which'll help keep his insolvency at bay for a few more months.'

'Is Sabi in debt?' asked Lizzie.

'Yeah. It's well known, he lost everything in the recession. And these palaces don't just look after themselves,' said Vona. 'Anyway, I must be getting ready for my next scene. Just have to make sure that that pig Romesh keeps his hands to himself. He's a dirty one, I tell ya, honey… Enjoy your time in India!'

She flashed Lizzie a perfect smile, and moved back out into the crowd. She was quickly joined by the boy with the umbrella who struggled along behind her, attempting to keep her shaded. Lizzie saw the actress start talking to a wealthy-looking Indian couple, who she guessed might also be spectators. Or perhaps they were *family*.

Soon the scene was wrapped and Lizzie was able to go back to the elephants, where Dick was sharing a joke with Pandu and the other riders. After a moment's reflection, she screwed up her resolve and beckoned Pandu to come over to her, away from the others.

'Give my love to your lady friend!' exclaimed Dick as Pandu signalled he was going. 'Don't do anything I wouldn't do...'

The other riders laughed as Pandu came over to her.

'I have to get back to my mum and dad now,' said Lizzie, when they were out of earshot. 'Look – I know it sounds weird, but I think I've seen someone who fits the description of the Pisaca – an English woman. Can you be around Dashashwamedha ghat early tomorrow morning? I think there's a good chance she might be there, that's where I saw her before. I'll be there too. We can follow her and see what she does.'

Pandu nodded eagerly. 'Of course,' he said. 'But stay around a bit longer – I'll take you back to your hotel.'

'No – I've really got to get back now. I'm late already. My parents'll kill me.'

'I'll cancel my next scene. Someone else can handle Ramses, I'll walk you back. It's dangerous, remember.'

'No – don't worry. Just give me directions, and I'll stick to the main streets.' She would have loved an escort after the encounter with the women, but knew it was impossible.

Pandu gave her the directions, but still looked worried.

'I'll be all right, honest,' Lizzie said, feeling anything but. 'Just be there early tomorrow – and wait for me. I could be a while, but I'll come. At Dashashwamedha.'

She hurried off through the film crew, out into the bustling streets of Kashi. For the first time, she was pleased there were so many people about.

*

'Have you found that damned priest yet?'

On the lantern-lit steps of the Kali temple the young priestess, Lamya, scowled as the three men shook their heads. Two were middle-aged and poorly groomed, but the third was young and clean shaven, with dark glasses and a large mole by his ear. It was the young man who spoke.

'One of our informants thinks she saw him at the scene of the Mistress's last victim,' he said. 'She said he was dressed as a ragged Pasupata, with his beard grown long. She knew him before, so was sure it was him.'

'Idiot! I don't want to hear he's been *seen*. What good is that?' shouted the woman. 'I need him caught! Get out, keep searching until you find him. And bring him back alive!'

The men rocked their heads in unison.

'Yes, Priestess,' said one of the older ones, a portly man with grey stubble and missing teeth. The men turned and hurried off down the street.

Shaking her head in frustration, the small woman grabbed one of the lanterns and strode back into the inner sanctum. *How would they ever succeed with fools like these?* At least Hanu was doing his job well, keeping track of those coming through the tirtha.

At the back of the sanctum she set the lantern down at the foot of the Kali effigy and knelt down. In the gloomy room, with the pale light of the lantern illuminating the gappy leer and nailed clubs of the old crone, Lamya dipped her head and began to pray.

She prayed that her mistress – the Pisaca, avatar of Kali herself – would come to her again tonight. *She needed her support now.*

She passed an hour like that, scarcely noticing the pain growing in her knees. Her mind fell into a sublime rapture, imagining over and over again the goals which she and her mistress and their companions were seeking. She imagined the ecstasy of transcending pallid, earthly limitations, and of having ever greater influence over the weak creatures of this world – and over the mysterious beings of the tirtha's world.

As she prayed, her lips trembled and she began to repeat in Hindi the words: 'Deliver us, Kali Ma, deliver us...'

And then there was a shift in the atmosphere, a dropping and a rising of the temperature, a shearing of the darkness. Lamya opened her eyes and looked up in wonder at the statue above her, where the lidless eyes shone with renewed, ultraviolet light.

Behind her, the priestess heard the sound of footsteps. Breathlessly she turned, to face the cloaked form of her mistress...

Chapter 10:   The Ride

The boy had never seen real snow before.

With his eye against a small hole in the cabin door, he watched as the grizzled flakes drifted down softly between slender, ivory-barked trees. He was bitterly cold, but as the snow sealed the forest floor with a carpet of white he thought he'd never seen anything so breathtakingly beautiful.

The boy yawned and stretched his aching limbs, only partially warmed by the layers of cardboard, straw and plastic in which he'd slept. Fitfully, he rummaged through his bright red bag of provisions. He'd found the bag in a ditch of tipped rubbish, and filled it with things he'd gathered in his night raids on the food shop and outlying farms and houses. He had a delicious pastry like a samosa, some vegetables, and a few pieces of bread which though dry were still softer than the chapatti back home. Best of all were some fresh bananas and a very sweet pastry, which he'd found wrapped in a paper bag in an isolated house a short way from the village. The owner hadn't seemed to be home, and the boy had snatched the bag through a window left tantalisingly ajar.

Occasionally some of the food made his stomach hurt, but he thanked Shiva he'd not been sick. *Yet.*

The boy had stumbled across the cabin the night before. It was yet another of the empty barns and buildings he kept discovering as he roamed the woods and fields under cover of the dark. He found it hard to believe how the Pisaca's people let so many good buildings go to waste. At home, in the countryside, people would soon repair them and fill them with their families and animals. He also found it hard to believe just how few of the demon's followers there were in this place, how *empty* the land was. At least that was something to be grateful for.

The cabin was small and cold, with lots of broken panels, but it was well-hidden, and warmer than being out in the open. And it felt much safer than the barn full of straw bales in which he'd been surprised by the terrifying white ogre, coming at him with its two-pronged trident.

The boy ate the remainder of the thing like a samosa, and sipped from his plastic bottle of water, filled from the local stream. Afterwards he sucked on the edge of a small piece of deliciously sweet and creamy chocolate he'd found dropped in the village. He felt his sluggish, demoralised spirits lift a little.

He stopped shuffling as a creature from the forest moved into his field of vision.

It was a fox, reddish fur ablaze against the snow. The creature dipped its snout cautiously to the ground as it advanced, and lowered its ears against its neck. Its soft, orangey tail flicked about, as its forepaws delicately tested the crust of snow.

After a few seconds, the fox stopped its search and jerked its head towards the hut. The boy froze as the ears pricked and – even through the tiny hole in the wooden panel – the feral eyes fixed on his.

He should have been scared, but wasn't. There was something about the animal that reassured him. It seemed gentle, almost serene, and he sensed instinctively that it didn't mean him any harm.

The fox stayed sitting in the snow watching the boy for a while, then it blinked and trotted off through the trees.

The boy stood up, and stretched his achy legs. He opened the door and headed out into the snow, to continue his hunt for food.

*

Bit by bit, a muffled conversation penetrated up through the house into Lizzie's slumber. Fleetingly, she thought she should wake herself up properly, but then the comfort and softness of bed won out…

'Lizzie!'

She opened her eyes.

'Lizzie!' Her mum was coming up the stairs. A moment later the door flew open.

'That was her *ladyship*, come to take you riding. You know, like you agreed – without my permission? I told her you were still in bed. At ten-thirty! She couldn't believe it. What's wrong with you these days?'

'Don't know,' Lizzie said, rubbing her tousled hair. 'Just tired. What did you tell her?'

'I said she'd better go without you.'

'You didn't!'

'Yes, I did – but she said she'd call back later,' said her mum. '*She's such a lovely girl,*' she added, mimicking Eva's deep, European accent.

'Leave it out, Mum,' Lizzie snapped. She *was* tired, and cross, too. *She was doing too much.* And now she'd gone and arranged to meet Pandu that night – *well, morning…*

As soon as her mum left, the anxieties of the night before returned. Who were those strange women, the *drav*-whatevers? What did they want from her? Surely there must be some connection between them and the Pisaca. And… *was* Ashlyn the Pisaca?

The evidence was building up. She was using the portal to Kashi. Like the child killer, she wore a cloak. And now Raj had confirmed someone else had seen a white woman with red hair near one of the killings. But, if she was the killer, why was she doing it? The only thing Lizzie could imagine was that she might be working with this terrible Kali cult. Perhaps, as Pandu said, that was where the black-skinned women had come from. Despite the warmth of her bed, she shuddered. *There was something so strange, inhuman, about them.*

Besides following Ashlyn with Pandu, she wondered if there was anything else she could do. It was pointless telling the police here in England – she could already see them dismissing her as a time-wasting kid with an overactive imagination. And she now knew she couldn't tell her mum about it. Things had gone too far, there was too much to explain. Even if her mum did believe her, she'd probably tell Godwin, or bring in other people and ruin the secret of the portal. Which would be terrible, especially if Ashlyn turned out *not* to be the killer. Lizzie had an increasingly strong sense that the portal was somehow *meant* for her – it was her own special secret to explore. As she had that thought, she imagined her great-uncle smiling down on her…

Taking a deep breath, she decided that, despite her worry about meeting the strange women again, following Ashlyn with Pandu was the right thing to do. *When everything's confusing,* as her dad used to say, *go with your guts.*

'What is it with you at the moment?' said her mum, as Lizzie shuffled past on her way to the kitchen. She was sitting on the sofa with her legs up, reading a copy of a woman's magazine. Lizzie could tell she was in a bad mood. *Perhaps Godwin had snubbed her.* 'Sleeping in every day, going round like you've got a secret or something.'

'I haven't,' Lizzie said, startled to think her expression might be giving something away. 'I'm just starting to get used to it here. It's… OK.'

'There's a turnaround. Before we left it was like we were going to the end of the earth.' Her mum thought for a moment and said: 'You haven't gone and got a boyfriend, have you?' She grinned. 'It's not that Thomas is it? His mum said you'd seen him the other day, in the fields.'

'Thomas! Who do you think I am?'

Her mum raised her eyebrows and looked down at her magazine. 'Well, I know it's something. I haven't been your mother these past thirteen years without learning to read you like a book.'

After lunch, Lizzie went out to play tug-o-war in the thawing snow with Tubs. She dropped to her knees and flicked powder at him, and he pranced about trying to catch it in his jaws. Lizzie giggled as he became increasingly frustrated and spattered with white flecks. Eventually she lunged forward and embraced him in a hug. Tubs swept his nose up across her chin and gave her a couple of licks, as if to show he knew it was a game all along.

After a while she began to feel the cold and headed back into the study to warm up with the dog in front of the fire. As she was sitting on her knees stroking Tubs' side, she noticed that an entire bookshelf beside the desk was empty.

That was odd, she thought, given that space elsewhere was so precious books had been crammed on top of one another, and were even two deep in places. *Perhaps her great-uncle had loaned some of his books to someone?*

She got up and began to browse through a shelf of Indian books. She flicked through one with pictures of Kali, with her necklace of skulls and different cutting weapons in her numerous hands. She noticed that the goddess had a variety of incarnations, from a fierce young woman to a toothless old crone.

As she was pushing the book back into the shelf, she spotted a small book entitled *Shiva's Holy City of Light*. She pulled it out and collapsed back into the tatty leather armchair. She began to read.

Someone – presumably her great-uncle – had taken a pencil furiously to the pages, underlining passages and marking paragraphs with exclamations, the most overused of which was simply *Yes!* Much of the book was about Kashi as a holy *tirtha*, the Indian name for a sacred crossing place, where gods and other supernatural beings could come down on to earth. Lizzie skimmed one section that was scored particularly heavily, about Kashi being the most sacred tirtha and being *present in many places at once.*

Her great-uncle had underlined the last phrase three times, and in the margin he'd written in his spindly, near-illegible scrawl: *garden = tirtha nexus, like Kashi?? cf Watkin's ley lines.*

Lizzie thought. Surely this confirmed what she'd suspected – that her great-uncle was using the portal – or *tirtha* – to Kashi? She looked out of the window, and remembered Mr Barrow mentioning Evelyn's friend, Alfred Watkins, who discovered ley lines. Did her great-uncle believe in them too? What did that word *nexus* mean?

Suddenly there was a knock on the front door and Mr Tubs began barking. Lizzie looked at the clock above the fire and saw it was nearly two o'clock – surely Eva come back for the riding session.

'I'll get it,' Lizzie shouted, going out into the hall. 'Tubs! Shut up!' she said, dragging the dog back from the door. But he kept on yapping, trying to push in front of her. She shoved him backwards with her foot and opened the door.

It was Eva, dressed in her green quilted waistcoat and riding boots. Her thick hair was tied up at the back of her neck and, without any make-up, her face looked handsome, almost masculine.

'He's perky,' she said, looking at the small dog. 'What's his name?'

'Mr Tubs,' said Lizzie, adding: 'He's not normally like this. *Tubs!*'

'He must be able to smell my spaniels,' said Eva, smiling as Lizzie slid him away into the study and slammed the door.

'I hear you've been having a lie-in,' Eva said.

Lizzie looked down, embarrassed. 'Yes, sorry,' she said. 'I overslept.'

'Must be all this country air. Are you ready to ride? The horses are waiting.'

Lizzie nodded eagerly. Whilst she collected her boots and coat Eva went into the kitchen and told her mum where they'd be going, assuring her that Lizzie would be quite safe because the horse she was riding was one of the gentlest mares she'd ever known. As she listened to Eva talking, Lizzie felt excitement fizz through her like sherbet.

Lizzie had never been in an SUV before and, knowing how bad they were for the environment, felt a twinge of guilt at how much she enjoyed the elevated view. *Like the English equivalent of an elephant,* she thought mischievously. She looked over the hedgerows into the fields, now largely thawed of the sudden snowfall except for the odd corner where the sunshine couldn't reach.

As they drove they talked about the horses, which Eva kept in a stable on the outskirts of Hebley. She explained that she didn't own the stables, but paid rent to a local farmer for them. The farmer fed and groomed the horses when Eva was away, and his wife and seventeen-year-old daughter helped to exercise them. She told Lizzie that the horses needed at least two hours' exercise a day, and that she took them out for their first ride just after sunrise.

'Even in winter?' asked Lizzie.

'Yep,' said Eva. 'Dressed in so many layers you wouldn't know there was a woman underneath.'

They drove into the stable courtyard and parked by a low, black shed with a corrugated roof. After they'd climbed out, Eva opened the car boot and produced two black riding hats. She helped Lizzie to fasten hers, then took her into one of the large stables where the horses, Manson and Isobel, were kept.

Lizzie had been excited about seeing the horses, but she hadn't expected to be *awed* by them. Manson was the great, shivering gelding she had seen Eva riding in Hebley. His body gleamed with health and power under the stable lights. Isobel was a compact, piebald mare, with soft brown eyelashes and a pink-white nose. As soon as she saw her, Lizzie fell in love. She could have stood and watched her all day.

'You remind me of when I rode my first horse,' said Eva.

'When was that?'

'A long time ago.' Eva laughed. 'In Poland. My father had one of the best stables in Eastern Europe.' At least now Lizzie knew where her accent came from.

Next Eva helped Lizzie put on the saddle. As she did so, Lizzie noticed that her hand was still bandaged.

'Why did Manson bite you?' she asked.

'It was my own fault. I was giving him peppermints and tried to pick one out of his gum. He didn't mean it.'

Lizzie wasn't tall or strong enough to throw the saddle over Isobel's back, but she felt the mare's flank shaking as she fastened the girth under her belly. Afterwards, they led the horses out into the courtyard and Eva stopped to help her up into the saddle. Lizzie noticed the fresh, flowery smell of Eva's perfume again.

Initially Lizzie's foot twisted in the stirrup, and she slipped back awkwardly onto the ground. She felt acutely self-conscious as Eva's hand came up to support her back for the second attempt. But this time she vaulted safely into the saddle and, as she steadied herself and looked around, she felt a surge of joy at being on horseback again. *Ramses was good – but an elephant just wasn't the same*, she thought.

They rode Manson and Isobel out on to the road, then diverted on to a stony bridleway across the fields. A crust of snow still lay unthawed beneath the path's sheltering hedges. The horses snorted vapour trails as they walked, their hooves clopping rhythmically on the path. For a while they didn't speak at all, and Lizzie slipped into a relaxed reverie. Finally they emerged through a gate and out into the open fields, which glowed hazily in the afternoon sun. They began to trot, and then Eva turned in her saddle and asked Lizzie if she wanted to gallop.

At the City Farm in Croydon, Lizzie had trotted and cantered a lot, but the ménage was so pitifully small she'd only ever galloped a few times before, mainly on holiday in Devon with her dad. So she nodded eagerly at Eva, and both gave the horses their head. Manson and Isobel needed little encouragement.

At first Lizzie found it difficult adjusting to the horse's movement, and she struggled to find the right position. But gradually she relaxed and found her rhythm, and then she began to enjoy herself. With the cold air streaming against her face, it felt like the whole landscape was charged with brightness and energy. *It was as if she was flying.*

They thundered past a farmhouse, causing a gaggle of geese by a cattle pond to honk loudly. Clods of earth flew up from Manson's hooves as the gelding sped ahead of Isobel. At one stage, Isobel's stride faltered and Lizzie was afraid the horse might fall, but then she was steady again and once more pounding the fields away beneath her.

Finally they saw Hoad's Wood and dropped back into a canter. As they approached the edge of the trees they slowed the horses to a trot and then stopped.

Lizzie could see the sweat steaming from Isobel's flanks.

'What about that?' said Eva.

'Fantastic!' said Lizzie. 'It felt as if she enjoyed it too.'

'These two love a good gallop. There's nothing like making your horse work.'

They fell into an easy conversation as they trotted along, talking about the horses Eva had owned.

'Which was your favourite?' asked Lizzie.

'What – you mean after this one?' said Eva, rubbing Manson's black mane. She drew in breath. 'That would be Mrok.' Lizzie frowned, and Eva laughed. 'Short for Mrok Blyskawica, which is Polish for *Dark Lightning*,' she explained. A distant look came into her eyes. '"A coat like a winter's night, eyes gentle as a doe's." That's what the famous Count Zaluski said about him. He made me quite an offer for him – but I turned it down.'

'Is that where you come from then - Poland?'

'Yes, I grew up there. But I've lived all over the world. Morocco, Romania, South America. I guess you could call me a nomad.'

'Have you ever been to India?' As soon as she said the words, Lizzie felt her cheeks burning. *Big mouth.*

Eva looked at her. 'Yes,' she said. 'All over, it's one of my favourite countries. Why – have you been?'

'No,' said Lizzie, quickly. Feeling like a fool, she wracked her mind for something else to say, to divert Eva's penetrating gaze from her face. After a moment she blurted: 'You don't seem old enough to have moved around so much.'

'I'm older than I look!'

'When did you come here?'

'Three years ago. I've always loved England, and was starting to feel I needed somewhere to settle. I wanted to live in the countryside, close to nature, and I fell for Herefordshire. There's no planes or motorways, it's hardly touched by the modern world. But enough about me – tell me about yourself.'

Lizzie shrugged. 'There's not much to say, really. I was brought up in London, born there. I don't have any brothers or sisters. We – me and my mum – lived in a flat in Croydon with my gran before we came down here. And I – just sort of… go to school, really.'

'No special experiences then?'

Lizzie frowned. 'Like – what?'

'You seem like a special girl to me. I'm sure you have lots ahead of you, like your great-uncle.'

'How well did you know him?' asked Lizzie, keen to get the subject off herself.

'Not half as well as I'd have liked,' said Eva. 'He came round to the Manor a few times, and we had

161

some fascinating conversations. Most often about his adventures with primitive tribes, like the Yanomami of Brazil. I remember some of his words to this day: *"They were subsumed within the natural order of things – the call of the macaw, the blinking of a tapir – and in turn they subsumed the natural order of things within themselves. For them, life and death weren't alternate states, but somehow one and the same."* He was like a poet.' She sighed, and added: 'He was a genuine polymath, he loved so many things besides anthropology. Fishing, philosophy, vintage cars, art, gardening. The list went on.'

'Yes,' said Lizzie, glancing up uncertainly. 'I love his garden.'

'Not such a big piece of ground,' said Eva. 'But he - and before him, his aunt - did so much with it. It's such a great idea, to theme it as a kind of World Garden. With all those rooms representing different cultures, times, and beliefs. Have you been exploring it?'

'Yes.'

'Found anything interesting?'

'Um – well, yes…'

'Like?'

'Well – lots of things. All those statues and sculptures. But… nothing else,' Again, she could feel her face burning. *Should she open up to Eva?* She felt a

162

sudden urge to, but didn't feel quite ready. *Perhaps next time.* She needed to think what to say.

After a moment of silence, Eva commented on how good Lizzie was at handling the horse. 'Did you learn everything you know at the City Farm?' she asked.

'Most of it,' said Lizzie. 'But my gran also paid for me to have some lessons after...' She stopped, her voice constricting with emotion. Noticing her distress, Eva reached out and touched her arm.

Lizzie swallowed, and finished: 'After my dad died.'

Eva's eyes softened with concern. 'I'm sorry. I didn't know. How long ago was that?'

'Just over a year.'

'You poor thing! That must have been awful.'

Lizzie glanced at the white sun, which was sinking towards the horizon. She smudged a tear from her cheek.

'Lizzie?'

'Mum says he was having an affair. But it's not true! She was just angry, because he hadn't got everything right, like proper insurance and stuff, and we lost the house...' Her eyes felt as if they were betraying her, filling with tears. She should have got over this by now. She was thirteen! *What would Eva think?* She looked away across the fields.

Eva drew alongside her on Manson, and took hold of her hand. 'You've obviously been through a lot, for someone so young,' she said. 'But what's important is that you loved your dad. And I bet he loved you, very much.'

Lizzie felt a release of tension and realised she wasn't, as she'd feared, going to cry. She looked round at Eva and gave a small nod.

'If you ever need anyone to talk to, you know where I am,' said Eva. 'I know how lonely it can be in a new place.' Then she added: 'I think you and I will be good friends.'

'I'd like that,' said Lizzie, as they turned their horses back towards the village. And then a guilty thought flashed through her head:

Why couldn't her mum be more like Eva?

Chapter 11:   The Festival of Lights

Lizzie was woken by a beeping at midnight.

Earlier she'd found a small digital clock in a cupboard in her mum's bedroom, and set its alarm. As soon as she turned it off, she sat up and looked out of the window.

The snow had come again, falling in thick white flakes across the garden and woods. It was starting to settle, brightening the dark ground. Under normal circumstances she loved snow but now, with the thought of what she was planning to do, just looking at it made her shiver.

She dressed in her warm clothes, picked up the torch and a reel of black cotton she'd found in a kitchen drawer, and hurried downstairs to the study. She blocked Mr Tubs from coming through – all she needed was for him to start barking – and unlocked the outside door. Then she perched on a stool beside the armchair, where she could duck out of sight if necessary.

She waited.

Resting her chin on her knees, she thought about the scrawled note in her great-uncle's book suggesting the garden might be a *tirtha nexus*, like Kashi. What did he mean by that? Perhaps he meant that the portal was like one of the Hindu's *sacred crossing places*. Did ley lines really exist, and one of them stretch all the way from Hebley to Kashi? She liked the word *tirtha*, and thought she would start to use it. But what did that word *nexus* mean? She wished she had a notebook to look it up. Then she thought about a dictionary. There must be one somewhere in the study.

She was just standing up to start searching when the sound of footsteps came down the side of the house. She crouched down again and held her breath as the darkly-clad intruder swept past the windows.

After a moment's silence, she dared to peek up above the window sill. Ashlyn had disappeared, so she jumped up and opened the door as quietly as she could. She knew the handle would make a noise, but had to take a risk if there was any chance of keeping up with the witch.

Outside it was freezing, with the snow settling fast. Turning on the torch, she could see the dim outline of Ashlyn's footprints crossing the lawn. Cold wet flakes blew against her face as, with a strange sense of foreboding, she followed the prints into the Indian garden and through to the statue of Shiva.

And, for the fourth time, she grasped the bronze ring of flame and walked counter-clockwise round the god to enter the City of Light…

*

In the underground chamber, she quickly stashed her coat on the edge of the well, and made her way out using the thin ledge to keep dry. As she was ascending the steep steps, she spotted a dark shape above her in the gloom and froze.

It only took her a moment to realise it was a cloak, carefully bundled up on the side of the stairs by the exit. She didn't have time to stop and examine it, so carried on out into the daylight.

As soon as she emerged on to the ledge she heard the crowd.

Hurrying to the corner of the building, she saw the Dashashwamedha ghats teeming with thousands of people, all struggling towards the river's edge. Giant wooden parasols and gaily-painted banners jostled above heads as people spilled into the murky water of the Ganges. The sound of horns and shouting filled the air. Lizzie wondered if she was witnessing some kind of stampede or mass panic, but everything seemed orderly enough.

She didn't have time to ponder. Looking down at the nearby walkway, she spotted Ashlyn in a black T-shirt and indigo jeans, striding in between the Indians. People were throwing her curious looks but she carried on regardless, heading up the steps towards the Old Town.

Lizzie jumped off on to the ghat and ran after her. Hanu was there, sitting on a propped platform under his umbrella, but he remained silent, watching her steadily as she went past. Feeling nervous, she avoided his gaze.

But when she reached the top of the ghats and looked around all she could see was the mass of people making their way down towards the river. She rushed into them, avoiding elbows and ignoring curses. She nearly tripped a woman carrying a basket with chicks in it. The woman yelled angrily at her. When Lizzie finally reached the end of the street she stopped, her chest heaving. She looked left and right, but Ashlyn was nowhere to be seen. Which way had she gone?

She began to feel a burning sense of frustration, when a familiar voice shouted:

'Lizzie! Over here!'

She looked round and saw Pandu at the entrance to one of the alleys. She ran over to him.

'Down here!' he said. 'She was heading back to the ghats. Come on!'

When the alley veered sharply to the right they stopped and peered around the corner. They briefly saw the witch silhouetted against the blue sky at the end of the passage, before she disappeared down a flight of steps.

'Why did she come up from the ghat only to go back down again?' whispered Lizzie.

'Perhaps she knows someone might be following her?'

The teenagers dashed to the end of the alley, and were just in time to see Ashlyn go into a large, five-towered temple below them.

'The Lakshmi temple...' said Pandu.

'Who?'

'Lakshmi. Goddess of wealth and good fortune. Diwali is her day, it's why everyone is here. She's a very popular deity.'

'Not surprised, with that portfolio,' said Lizzie, feeling momentarily pleased with herself for using an expression she'd heard but not used before. 'What shall we do now?'

'Well, we can't follow her in.'

'Why not?'

'There aren't many rooms inside – they'd see us.'

Pandu thought for a moment, looking at the building. Then he said: 'Wait here. Make sure she doesn't see you if she comes back out.' He ran to the nearest tower and began to climb, using the animal and flower carvings as grips.

'Pandu!' shouted Lizzie. 'Don't! That's dangerous!'

He looked round at her. 'Shhh! She'll hear you!'

He carried on climbing, seemingly devoid of fear, and soon he was high up and inching around to the one window in the ochre tower. Lizzie saw him peer in, then he looked down at her and shook his head. Next he shuffled around the edge of the tower into the middle of the roof, where the central tower rose like a giant bishop's hat, encrusted with carved statuettes. He hopped on to it and peered in through one of the glassless windows. There he remained, watching and listening for what seemed like ages.

Lizzie fidgeted with her pony tail, finding the waiting unbearable. What could he see? *What was Ashlyn doing in there?* After a while she heard a chuckle below her, followed by a sharp cry. Looking down, she saw that a burly man with close-cropped hair had spotted Pandu, and was shouting to his colleagues seated a few steps down from him.

Pandu glanced down from the tower. Lizzie could see the anger on his face, but there was nothing he could do except turn back and continue watching. The men got to their feet and came up to their colleague. They began shouting too.

Lizzie knew she had to do something before everyone started looking up. She hurried down the steps towards the men, saying: 'Hey! Excuse me – does anyone here know the way to the Marble Palace?'

They all looked around, an English girl on her own being marginally more interesting than a boy on a roof. Two of the three didn't seem to be able to understand English, but one had a reasonable grasp.

'Where again do you want to go?' he asked. He had thin, black-framed glasses and was quite handsome, in a sharp-looking way. Lizzie thought he might be a student.

'The Marble Palace?'

At that moment the stocky man grabbed her arm and pointed up at Pandu, saying something in Hindi.

The bespectacled man started to laugh. 'He said, "do you see the monkey on the roof?"'

'Very funny,' said Lizzie, looking disapprovingly at the man. 'But where's the palace?'

'Who are you?' asked the young man. His eyes were very dark, and he had a large brown mole just below his left ear.

'My name's Rowena. I'm English and I need to get to the palace. My father's the ambassador, and he's meeting with Sabi.' She lifted her jaw slightly, trying to affect an air of entitlement.

The young man smiled thinly and said something in a low voice to his friends, who began grinning at her, making her feel uncomfortable. She was sure the man didn't believe her story. Nevertheless he began to give her stilted directions, all the while glancing up at Pandu. His colleagues carried on chuckling and chatting, bemused both by the 'ambassador's daughter' and the boy scuttling over Lakshmi temple like a spider. *At least she'd succeeded in stopping them making such a racket.*

Lizzie also kept looking up to check Pandu was all right. After a while he inched back down from the window and climbed on to the nearby tower. She guessed Ashlyn must be coming out. But then a young woman with a small boy appeared on the ghat, and the child started screeching and pointing excitedly at the teenager as he clambered down. In the next moment, Ashlyn emerged through the temple doors, followed by a bearded old man in a loincloth. The man had a staff in his hand, and red lines marked on his cheeks.

After a moment of confusion, Ashlyn followed the direction of the child's pointing finger and spotted Pandu leaping off the tower on to the ghat. She said something to the old man, then headed off quickly down river.

The men with Lizzie started shouting again, and the one with the spectacles said:

'Who is she? Is she with you?'

Lizzie wasn't listening. She ran to Pandu and they both set off after Ashlyn. But as they came past the temple door the strange-looking old man shouted 'Stop!' and moved forward to block their way.

The children tried to dive around either side of him. The man swung his staff at Pandu's legs and the boy just managed to save his shins by leaping into the air. But he was unable to prevent himself landing badly on the edge of a step and there was a clunk as his knees and elbows struck stone. He cried out in pain.

Angrily, Lizzie turned back at the old man, now stepping down towards Pandu, and took a run at him. Before he could react she gave him a mighty shove, causing him to lose his footing. He tumbled awkwardly down the steps, his staff flying off through the air. He was a good way down before he finally managed to stop himself.

Lizzie grabbed Pandu by the arm. 'Are you all right?' she said.

'Yes,' he said, easing himself up. Lizzie saw he'd split the skin on both knees, and there was dust and gravel mixed in with the blood. She glanced at the old man, who was groaning and attempting to lever himself up. *Something about him looked familiar.*

'Where's the Pisaca?' asked Pandu, and they both looked down along the ghat. They could see Ashlyn moving into the fringe of the crowd around Dashashwamedha. 'Come on!' he said, and began to hurry after her, hobbling slightly.

'No!' said Lizzie, looking indecisively at the old man. She was torn between wanting to catch Ashlyn and help this strange figure whom she was sure she'd seen before. 'I think I've hurt him...'

Pandu stopped and glanced at the man. 'He tried to hit me!' he exclaimed, then added: 'He'll be all right – if we don't go after her now, we'll lose her!' He began to run after Ashlyn, awkwardly at first but quickly picking up speed.

Lizzie took one more uncertain look at the old man. His eyes seemed red and dazed, and there was something sad, almost pitiful about him. His cheeks were streaked with tears. But he'd managed to get back on his feet again, so she guessed he couldn't be too badly hurt.

Where had she seen him before?

'I'm sorry,' she called to him, and ran off after Pandu.

*

As the two young people disappeared into the crowd, the three men hurried down the steps to the old priest. The one with the black-rimmed glasses helped him to stand up straight, whilst the burly one collected his staff from where it had fallen.

'Are you all right, baba?' asked the one with the glasses and mole.

The old man, whose head felt like it was stuffed with cushions, blinked to improve his focus. Everything he could see and hear seemed mixed up, and the steps in front of him appeared to be tilting diagonally. But despite his confusion, he had the sense to realise he was probably only concussed.

'I'll be all right,' he said. 'I just need to sit down.'

'You've a nasty gash on the side of your head, baba,' said the young man. 'Here, we'll help you.'

'I think I need to sit down for a while,' the priest repeated.

'Come and sit up there,' said the man, gesturing to the top of the ghat.

'Why not here?'

'Because I said so – *Bakir*,' said the man with glasses and at that moment, despite the cloudiness in his head, the priest understood the full depth of cruelty in the man's eyes.

'Leave me alone…' he began.

'Baba!'

Everyone looked up to see a skinny caretaker boy standing in the doorway of the temple, mop in hand.

'Are you all right?' the boy called out, in a loud voice.

'He's OK – we're just helping the priest. One of those kids knocked him down,' said the third man with the group, who was wearing red pyjamas. He began climbing the steps towards the boy.

'Nalin – run! Run for help!' shouted the old priest.

The burly man who'd picked up the priest's staff struck him hard on the back of the skull with it, and he collapsed on to the ghat.

'Baba!' shouted the boy again, anxiously. He watched in panic as the man in pyjamas approached him. The man was grinning, revealing several missing front teeth. He was quite old, with grey stubble and bloodshot eyes, but his open, gappy smile made him look peculiarly youthful. He seemed to be scratching his side as he approached the cleaning boy.

'Don't panic, friend – we're only helping the priest.'

Then the boy noticed what the man had been rummaging for at his side: a short, curved dagger.

'No!' he cried, staggering back into the temple.

*

As they pushed through the crowd, Pandu had to keep hoisting Lizzie up so she could spot Ashlyn. The witch was making her way towards the Old Town, which was still thronging with people eager to reach the ghats.

'What's everyone doing?' asked Lizzie.

'As I said, it's a festival day,' replied Pandu. 'Tonight they'll light candles on saucers and send them out across the river – for anyone who needs good fortune.'

'Sounds like us…' muttered Lizzie, as they pushed forward through the masses.

In the Old Town, Ashlyn headed into an alley off one of the main streets. The teenagers were just in time to see her pushing awkwardly past an irate group of pilgrims carrying a golden effigy of Lakshmi.

'We won't catch her that way – quick, let's try and cut her off!' said Pandu.

But by the time they'd followed a circuitous route round to where the witch should have come out, she was nowhere to be seen. They hurried down a few less crowded alleys, but there was no sign of her.

'Damn!' exclaimed Pandu, sitting down on a stack of broken pallets propped against a wall. An olive billboard hung above him, filled mostly with Hindi script but ending in a picture of a packet of crisps and an English caption: *"Bitos – Full of snack and cracky Fun!"*

Lizzie sat down beside him. 'You need to get those cuts cleaned,' she said.

But Pandu was deep in thought. 'I didn't get much of what she said to the priest,' he said after a moment. 'Her voice was too low. But his was louder, and I heard him mention the Lingam.'

'The what?'

'The Lingam,' repeated Pandu. 'The holiest symbol of Shiva. There was one here in the Blue Temple, but it was stolen a few days ago. Everyone's been worried about it. It's believed to protect the city. They think there might be a connection between the Pisaca and its disappearance.'

'What did the old man say about this *Lingam*?'

'It sounded like he might know where it is – but he didn't tell her. I think... I think he was saying something about keeping it safe. He said it had *wounded* the Pisaca – but I didn't hear how. Then he said something about being followed by Kapilikas, worshippers of Kali. And then he asked her something about 'the child', and whether he was still safe. I heard her say she was *leaving things out for him*, whatever that meant. But then the cleaning boy came in and they went into the inner sanctum, where I couldn't hear them anymore.'

Lizzie thought for a moment, then said: 'If that's true then he didn't think Ash... *she* was the Pisaca.' She felt herself blush, but Pandu didn't seem to notice.

'No.'

'What are we going to do now?'

'I don't know,' said Pandu.

'I think we should go back and look for the priest. He must be able to tell us more. And I'm sure I've seen him somewhere before.'

'OK,' said Pandu. 'But if he has a swipe at me again, I'll knock his block off.'

'I just hope I didn't hurt him when I pushed him over,' said Lizzie then, glancing at Pandu's legs, she added: 'Let's clean that up before we go.'

Pandu asked a woman going into a nearby house to give them a cup of water, then Lizzie crouched down and washed the scabbed blood off.

'There's a lot of grit in it, you need disinfectant,' she said, rubbing as hard as she dared with her hanky. Pandu winced. 'They're going to bruise nicely,' she added.

They began to head back on a route which avoided the pilgrims. As they walked, Lizzie noticed that Pandu had gone quiet. She asked him if his knees were still hurting.

'It's not that,' he said. 'It's… after what the priest said…I have another connection with the Blue Temple. My little brother lives and works there. Or *used* to. When our uncle died I was taken in by the priests of the Ganesh temple, and my brother went there.'

'How long ago was that?'

'Three years,' said Pandu. He looked at her, and in the weak morning sunlight she noticed the sadness in his eyes. 'My parents were killed in a train crash seven years ago, when my brother and I were staying with our uncle on his farm.'

'Oh no…'

'They were coming back from a visit to the Taj Mahal, to celebrate their wedding anniversary. After that, we lived with our uncle, helping him out on his farm. We had to work really hard, getting up before dawn to milk the cows and goats before we went to school. And Uncle Devi had bad lungs, so we had to do more and more as time passed. But he was devout, and before he died he got us positions in the temples.'

'Did you still see your brother afterwards?' asked Lizzie. She'd always wished she'd had a brother. *How awful to have one and lose him.*

'Not much. Neither of us had much time. We were still close, but life in the temples is hard too, especially with school on top. *And* when you're looking after a fully grown elephant.'

'When did your brother…'

'Disappear? Only a few days ago. A friend told me, his father read it in the paper. They say he was taken by the Pisaca. But he's not dead, I know it – and I'm going to find him. I knew Raj already, he's a relative – a second cousin on my mother's side – and I pestered him to let me help with the investigation. I told him I'd do it alone unless he let me.'

'And he agreed?' said Lizzie, incredulously.

'Reluctantly. And as long as I stay out of trouble.'

'Could there be a connection between what the old priest said – about the Lingam – and your brother's disappearance? It's got to be more than just coincidence that they were both at the same temple, and disappeared at the same time. I wonder what the priest had to do with it?'

'From the way he was talking, it sounded as if he might have come from the Blue Temple, too,' said Pandu, frowning.

'Maybe there's a link with the Kali followers?' said Lizzie.

'There could be,' said Pandu, and shuddered.

They were now in the heart of the Old Town, making their way through a maze of tight alleyways packed with street vendors, beggars, and travellers. Stalls selling beads, flowers, herbs, and henna were crammed into nooks and doorways. In the air sweet-scented perfumes – sandalwood, jasmine, and lavender – competed with the smells of exotic spices and cooking. Dodging people, drains and untidy stalls, Lizzie began to feel increasingly claustrophobic. Again she became aware of furtive glances. She reached forward and took hold of Pandu's arm.

'Look!' he said suddenly, pointing down an alley.

Following his gaze, Lizzie saw a higgledy-piggledy complex of buildings surrounding a magnificent blue dome with a trident at its peak. At the arched entrance of the complex, priests in white robes stood guard.

'That's it,' said Pandu. 'The Blue Temple.'

'Ask the guards if there's any more news of the Lingam,' said Lizzie.

Pandu did, but from the miserable expressions on the priests' faces Lizzie could tell that there wasn't.

*

In the temple of Kali, the priestess Lamya shivered with excitement as the inner sanctum grew momentarily cold and its candles flickered wildly, highlighting the axes and poking blades clasped in the hands of the statue before her. Lamya turned to see a dark cloaked figure coming across the flagstones.

'Mistress,' she said, dropping to her knee.

'Stand,' croaked the figure.

The priestess stood and looked up at the distorted face, hidden within the hood. All she could make out was a heavy jaw, swollen with fangs.

'I hear you have news?'

'Yes – we've captured the priest Bakir,' said the priestess. The proud smile dropped from her face as the cloaked figure advanced quickly and towered above her.

'How?'

'My agents spotted him in his disguise as a Pasupata, and followed him to the Lakshmi temple. He met someone there – the English witch. We caught him after she left, and put him in the chamber.'

'Excellent!'

'There's more,' said the priestess, looking up. 'The English girl was there too, with a street boy. The Daginis obviously weren't enough to frighten her off. The agents believe she was following the witch. I think we should find out what she knows – and soon. She might even know something about the Lingam.'

'You think so?'

'Perhaps. Bakir might have told the witch, who could have told the girl. Or perhaps the girl has found the temple boy who hid it, the one who escaped back in England.'

'It's possible,' said the hooded figure, then added: 'We *have* to find the Lingam. But it would be risky, removing someone on the other side – especially as she lives with her mother.'

'But as you said, the police there are in your palm.'

'England isn't India! The disappearance of a child could make national news. Before we knew it there'd be reporters flocking to the village, and they'd soon get wind of the so-called *Wild Boy* in the woods. We've done a good job of keeping that news local so far.'

'Maybe you could use the mother's new confidant to set up an accident? You could get rid of the mother, and bring the girl back here. Perhaps a car crash? We could always supply a body, which would suffice for the girl if the flames were hot enough.'

'If the priest doesn't talk I'll think about it. One way or another, we have to find the Lingam soon. The pull from the Realms is getting stronger all the time. Chen is translating the Book of Life, and we're starting to work out where the other artefacts are to operate the Fountainhead. But the Lingam is critical. If we're going to succeed, you must get that priest to talk.'

Chapter 12: In the Witch's Cottage

Deep in a candlelit underground chamber, Bakir lay tied to a stone slab.

For a while, time seemed to have no meaning for him as he drifted in and out of consciousness, surfing on the crest of his pain. He had encountered a real demon before – *the Pisaca* – but she'd been nothing compared to the man and woman alone with him now in this dark, forgotten cellar.

As Lamya stood and watched, Hanu had used iron implements to inflict unspeakable wounds on him. Bakir had never experienced such agony before, writhing on the plinth and screaming like a baby.

'Where is it? Where's the Lingam?' Lamya hissed, leaning close to his ear. 'Tell us, and it'll all be over, old man.'

Whereas before he'd seen softness in those small, nut-brown eyes, now he perceived only savageness and cruelty – all the worse for being contained in such a gentle-looking face.

For a while, Bakir lost his mind. He found himself back in school, surrounded by scrubbed, eager children in white shirts, sitting at wooden desks with their yellow HB pencils ready. Light poured into the classroom through four large windows, through which he could see the brown ridges of the Himalayan foothills in the distance. His favourite teacher, Mr Hayar, bald with a black-and-grey beard, moved among the children, talking in his cheery, sardonic voice. "See the trinity, the *Trimurti*," he was saying. "Brahma creates the world; Vishnu preserves the world; and Shiva destroys the world…" The children carefully transcribed his words on their feint-lined exercise books. "But don't worry about Shiva, children. His destruction is good destruction. If everything stayed the same forever, there'd be no place for the new. Imagine nothing new to see and feel and enjoy the world! Death is Nature's way of keeping life fresh…"

'You're talking in your sleep, baba,' said Lamya.

Bakir opened his eyes, and the safe, cocooned memory of childhood vanished as the pain returned. He noticed something new in the room – the acrid smell of coal burning. There was smoke in the air. 'And you are wrong, very wrong. Death is not our friend. Death, above all, is our enemy. Death will take every last piece of Nature to the Unknown Realms in the end. There

186

will be nothing left. Even Kali Ma does not want that. So some of us must fight it, and that means making some sacrifices along the way.'

Hanu grinned as he approached the old priest with a long metal poker, which glowed yellow at the tip.

*

The next morning, Lizzie wrapped herself up and hurried out to the entrance of the Indian garden. After checking that the black cotton she'd fastened across the entrance the night before was still there – indicating Ashlyn hadn't yet returned – she took Mr Tubs out through the wood and across the fields.

Bright herringbones of cloud raked the sky, disintegrating in the distance into patches of silvery-blue. A fresh snowfall had covered the fields, and the whiteness was broken only by a few solitary oaks and the odd black crow hopping about. In the distance, the mountains looked like giant sculptures of ice.

As she walked she couldn't stop thinking about the temple cleaner. When she and Pandu had finally got back to the Lakshmi temple, they'd found it cordoned off, with police all around. Pandu soon found out the boy had been stabbed by one of the men, and taken away to hospital.

Yet another innocent victim of this mystery, Lizzie thought miserably. Was there anything she and Pandu could have done to save him? *Perhaps if they'd gone straight into the temple, things might have worked out differently.* But one thing she was certain of – now she would do everything in her power to stop another child being killed. That was why she was going to Limetree Cottage, to see if she could find any clues there.

As she was walking, with Tubs running along behind her, she remembered where she'd seen the priest before. *He was at the scene of the first murder near the fountain.* He was the one who'd run out past the policeman, and turned the body of the girl over. What a terrible thing to do... Or maybe he was trying to see if it was someone he knew? She remembered his strange expression of relief when he first saw the girl's face, before he became angry.

Once again, she felt overwhelmed by the complexity of everything. *There was so much she didn't know.* She began to despair she'd ever be able to understand what was going on around her. But at least now she felt she had some help, from Raj and Pandu.

As she came into Hebley she forced herself to concentrate. She put Tubs on his lead and asked a couple of people for further directions. Soon she was out of the village and heading down a country lane in between snowy fringes of woodland. When she finally caught sight of Limetree Cottage, set back behind a high thorny hedge, she felt a flurry of nerves in her stomach. She reminded herself that the cotton trap was still intact, so the cottage's owner must still be in Kashi.

She reached the front gate and stopped. Tying Tubs' lead around one of the snow-capped gate posts she stroked his snout and said: 'Keep watch, boy.'

She opened the gate and crept up the cleared path to the small, creeper-strewn house. Her anxiety increased with each step. She glanced in through a window and saw a simple white room with wooden floors, a wood-burning stove, and shelves filled with books. There was an open book on a coffee table in front of a small green sofa. Otherwise, there was no sign of life.

She headed round the back, following the path down the side of the house. At the bottom of the long back garden she saw a dilapidated shed and a brook running off into the woods. A pile of rough-cut logs were scattered around a tree stump, with more stacked against the shed. A hatchet was stuck in one of the logs. Suddenly Lizzie noticed movement in the snow by the stream and then she spotted the slender back and tail of a fox, disappearing into the undergrowth. Like the one she'd seen in the Indian garden, it looked a lot healthier than the mangy street creatures back in Croydon.

Surveying the back of the house, she noticed the kitchen window was ajar. *Didn't they have burglars in the countryside?* she wondered. Whatever, it was good news for her. After another glance around, she pulled the window fully open, and peered inside.

The kitchen was small and darkly painted, with a pine table, two red chairs, and a picture of a seascape on the wall. Silver pans of various sizes hung on a rail above an old cooker. A half-open door led through to the lounge. Strangely, a load of fresh food – bread, biscuits and fruit – was piled on the worktop below the window ledge.

Lizzie reached in and, carefully checking how the food was arranged, pushed it aside. Then she hoisted herself up on to the windowsill, and climbed through on to the worktop. She swung her legs round, and dropped down onto the tiled floor. Heart thumping, she hurried through the half-open door into the living room.

Besides the open book on the table, she noticed a few dark green, abstract paintings in gilded frames on the walls, and a beautifully-made fox head mask hanging above the mantelpiece. Whilst she was drawn to the mask, Lizzie realised the book was more important and hurried over to it. As soon as she saw the dense, semi-legible scrawl she gasped – she knew her great-uncle's handwriting when she saw it.

'*10th December, 2003. Abena's young boy, Zuri, continues to cause trouble for the villagers. Over the last few days I have seen him strike a little girl half his age and blacken her eye; drop a handful of wet mud in the doro wat (making his mother have to throw it all away, showering him with endless curses whilst he smiled on disdainfully); throw a toy nkisi stick at another boy; and spend a whole afternoon shrieking in a manner which set everyone's teeth on edge (Abena tried to beat him into quietness, but failed entirely).*

I am surprised none of the men have taken him in hand. His father seems to have died of some rare disease or infection – they have no name for it, but it involved a great deal of unpleasant bleeding from the mouth, nose and ears – and, for some reason, the others prefer to leave the boy alone. It is as if they attribute him special licence, but I don't know why.

Every so often I have another go at trying to engage with him, and it's clear he is intelligent enough. He is happy working out card tricks or improving his English, and he has an amazing ability to hit a tree with a spear at ten yards. I suspect one day he will be a great hunter. But for now, like so many gifted children, he is easily bored – and when bored, Zuri tends towards destructiveness. I fear if he carries on like this there will come a time when the other villagers will have no option but to throw him out...'

Brilliant! Her great-uncle had kept a diary. *This was better than anything she'd hoped to find.* But how had Ashlyn got hold of it? Had he given it to her? *Or had she stolen it?* She glanced out of the window at the front gate. Like a good watchdog, Tubs was sitting looking up and down the road. Eagerly, she flicked to the back of the book and read another passage.

29th September 2005. Was allowed to observe the inma of David Maturwarra's oldest son, Richard, at the Two Boy boulders. The inma is an initiation ceremony into the story of the ancestors which takes place as soon as a boy is judged old enough to understand its lessons. The ceremony involved a great deal of dancing and clapping of sticks, presided over by an elder, who told Dreamtime stories of the Two Boys and the creation of Uluru. In the centre of the circle, Richard did his own little dance, his face carefully painted up by his sister.

Afterwards, David and I took a walk around Uluru and he told me about his journeys in dreamtime. The more I hear him speak of dreamtime – the 'eternal' time, more real for the Aborigines than the physical world – the more I am convinced I experience something similar in the moment of transportation through the tirthas.

David believes we live in a time of monumental change in the Spirit World, when the Archetypes are being drawn away to…

There! She finally had the confirmation that her great-uncle had used the portal – the *tirtha* – too.

And yet… She snatched up the diary and peered harder at the awful writing. She felt her skin crawl with goose bumps as she re-read 'through the *tirthas…*'

Was there more than one?

Images of the different gardens, with their statues and art works, flooded through her mind. *Was Kashi just one tirtha among many?* Had her great-uncle been able to undertake all those anthropological investigations just by stepping out of his back door?

For a moment she stood dumbfounded. Then she shook her head and forced herself to concentrate. *She could check the other rooms and their statues later.* Right now she needed to focus. She looked back at the diary, and checked the dates at the start and end: 13th June 2003 – 27th October 2005. *There must be more.* She looked around the room again and saw a neat stack of similarly bound leather journals on one of the bottom shelves, roughly the same size as the empty shelf in her great-uncle's study. *How many diaries had he written?*

She glanced at another paragraph:

Like so many of the holy men and mystics I have encountered around the world, David and the other Aborigines believe that beings from their ancient stories really exist, and sometimes come down on to Earth. These mythical beings – gods, angels, demons, all the lesser creatures – come from another plane, the dreamtime.

But the more I talk to mystics of differing cultures, the more I am convinced that their spiritual realms – the Christian heaven, the Buddhist Nirvana, the Hindu Atman – are all aspects of one plane, *interwoven with the fabric of our mundane reality. And what if such a unifying plane – which is not so dissimilar to the theories set out by modern physicists, with their 'action at a distance' – is the thing which connects the tirthas, and enables them to work? And, if that's so could it be, as David says, that mythical beings and creatures are* real, *and can come out into the world through the tirthas? If so, I pray that I meet one before I die…*

Lizzie looked up, her mind reeling. *Had her great-uncle really believed in gods and demons?* For a moment, the image of the three black-skinned women flashed in her mind. Maybe her instinct was right, and they really *weren't* human...

She shook her head – and froze as a metallic scraping sound came from the kitchen. *Someone was there.*

She considered hiding behind the sofa, but then thought again. If it was Ashlyn, surely Tubs would have barked? Even if the witch had come in through the woods at the back, she would have gone to the front door. Perhaps it was an animal, trying to get in the

194

window? *The fox?* Taking a deep breath, she peered round the edge of the door.

And found herself looking straight into the surprised face of a boy pressed against the window, his arm reaching in to grab the food. Lizzie noticed his shaggy black hair, sallow, pinched face, and ragged clothes. For a moment, as they held each other's eye, something seemed to pass between them – some glimmer of recognition, understanding – and then the boy turned and fled.

'No – stop!' Lizzie shouted, running to the window.

The boy was leaping the brook at the bottom of the garden, heading off into the woods. She rushed back into the living room and, without pausing to think, snatched one of the journals from the book shelf. Then, with the book under her arm, she opened the front door and ran to collect Tubs, who was bristling with excitement.

'Come on, Mr T – we've got to catch him!' she exclaimed, and ran off with the little dog through the garden and into the frozen woods.

*

No matter how much they hurt him, Bakir would never tell them what they wanted to know. They burnt the old priest on his chest and legs, but still he didn't say where he and the boy had hidden the Lingam.

After a while, seeing they were getting nowhere, they left him alone. Hanu told him he'd die and reincarnate as a termite, and Lamya told him he wouldn't succeed, that next they'd see how he responded to another kind of fear altogether. But he didn't reply. He was past caring, and grateful just to be left alone.

He lay moaning softly, staring at the shadows of the ceiling. He had passed a threshold, and instead of pain all he felt was emptiness. The only things he could hear were his own laboured breathing, and an occasional dripping of water.

He wasn't sure how long he lay there like that. It could have been hours, days, or perhaps only moments. He thought about the suffering welcomed by Shiva's more extreme Pasupata devotees - the self-inflicted piercings and mutilations - but wondered if any had endured anything like this. The Lord of the Dance had certainly chosen to test him to his limits. *And he, Bakir, would not fail him.*

He must have passed out for a while, because he came to with an overwhelming sense of dread. Anxious images from his dream – of the Pisaca hurling him into the river, of waking up alone on the bank, with Albi gone – flittered through his mind. He twisted his head round, but the room was empty. The candles in their holders were almost burnt down, their flames flickering wide and long as they approached the moment of extinction. He felt a momentary panic at the idea of being left alone in complete darkness. What if they never came back, and left him to starve to death?

But then the sound of footsteps came on the stairs. A quick tug on his bonds told him they were still tight, and made him realise how weak he was. He could scarcely move his fingers and toes. Even trying to made him feel sick.

Suddenly his panic returned. As the footsteps, heavier than Lamya's and Hanu's, came closer, he noticed a new odour in the air – something faintly metallic, rusty, like... *blood*. He was seized by a sense of impending catastrophe. It was the same unsettling smell he'd noticed a few days' ago, when the terrified Albi had led him to the holy well in the Blue Temple to show him who – or rather *what* – was trying to steal the Lingam...

Chapter 13:   The Temple of Kali

'I'm not having it anymore! You people don't even know how to begin to make a movie! *He* can't act to save his life because he's too pickled, and *he* can't keep his filthy paws to himself. I'm not having it!'

Vona Makkouk was referring to Dick Pike and Romesh Nagra respectively. Listening to the actress' third blow up of the day, Pandu slumped forward and idly scratched the peak of Ramses' head. The elephant snorted, irritable in the midday heat.

'I can't act? Oh, that's funny. That's really funny coming from a spoilt little brat like you,' said Dick. Romesh said nothing, but raked his fingers anxiously through his quiff.

They were filming the first marriage scene – scripted as *"Failed Marriage Scene #1"*, because Romesh was falsely accused of cheating with Vona's sister – down by the waterfront. A priest, splendid in burnt-orange robes, was blessing the characters with water from the Ganges. The whitewashed turrets of the palace rose up majestically in the background, freshly repainted by the film company.

'Don't you *dare* call me that, you pathetic old drunk!' shrieked Vona. Pandu, who'd lost interest a long time ago in the star's tantrums, watched as Ramses plugged his trunk into the river to take a drink.

'You think everyone's after you, don't you? That's why you spend so much time in front of the mirror, making yourself up,' said Dick. 'But one of these days you'll realise how attractive a little maturity is.'

'Please, please!' cried the director, a fat, middle aged man with a round face and neat white beard. 'It's getting hot, I think we all need a break! I'm going to call the rest of the day a holiday.'

'The sooner this stupid film is finished…' muttered Dick, as the crew and cast began to break up.

Grateful for the unexpected break, Pandu headed back towards the Temple of Ganesh to stable Ramses. As the elephant wended his way through the bustling streets the boy reflected on the morning's events, and particularly on Lizzie's mysterious disappearance into the underground chamber of the old temple. Fingering her watch in his pocket, he wondered if Amjad the Ironmonger would exchange it for a torch so he could explore the chamber. He'd thought about returning the watch, now he knew Lizzie – but decided against it.

Westerners could always afford to lose a few of their material possessions, and how else besides the odd bit of petty theft could he fund the small bribes and miscellaneous items he needed to make his investigations? *It was hardly as if he could sit in one of those new expensive cafes, straining to hear the hushed conversation of a pair of Kapilikas, without a coffee in front of him.*

He decided to give Raj a call on his mobile. Safely concealed beneath his tunic, the silver phone was his prize possession, given to him by the Inspector for safety and reporting back when scouting. He drew it out and dialled.

The Inspector answered before Pandu had even heard it ring. 'Pandu?'

'Yes Uncle. I've discovered another mystery. I followed the girl this morning and she didn't go back to the Rama. She went to an old disused temple at the end of Dashashwamedha. There was a hidden entrance out above the river, with steps going down into a dark, flooded room. There was no reply when I called, so I'm going to get a torch and go back for another look.'

'Odd,' said Raj. 'I'll come with you. But wait a bit, because I'm just coming back from the hospital, and have something else to do. The Lakshmi cleaning boy came round. He's a simple kid, but lucid about what happened. He says they were Kapilikas who kidnapped the priest.'

'Kapilikas! How did he know?'

'The priest told him they were after him. The priest and boy are friends, they've known each other for a long time. The priest was one of the resident brahmin at the Blue Temple, but something very bad happened a week ago and he went on the run. He was a normal Shiva priest, but he disguised himself as a wild Pasupata so they wouldn't find him.'

'What about the woman with the priest – the one we think's the Pisaca – did he know her?'

'He'd seen her a couple of times,' said Raj. 'She left notes with him to arrange meetings with the priest – in the same way that some old English chap used to do, apparently.'

'Why were the Kapilikas after the priest?' asked Pandu.

'He didn't know. But I intend to find out.'

'How?'

'I'm paying a visit to the Kali temple.'

'Can I meet you there? We could both go to the derelict temple afterwards.'

A moment's silence. 'I'm not sure.'

'Why?'

'I don't want you to be exposed to any risks. We agreed your involvement was to remain at the level of lookout. Things may start to get uglier now.'

'They've already got ugly for me,' said Pandu. 'Remember? I've lost my little brother.'

Raj considered for a moment. 'OK. But I'm bringing Sergeant Singh too.'

'I'm just taking Ramses back. I'll meet you there in twenty minutes.'

*

When he heard footsteps on the stairs Bakir, half senseless with his terrible wounds, prayed it wouldn't be the Pisaca again. For hours the demoness had tormented him, physically and mentally, and he knew he couldn't hold out much longer. He found himself almost longing for an easeful death.

But it wasn't the Pisaca. It was the Kali priestess, Lamya, and this time she didn't have the golden-eyed fool Hanu with her. She was on her own.

She had a small cloth bag with her, and she walked around the room, replacing the burnt-out candles in the wall holders.

'How are you feeling, my poor Pasupata?' she asked, as she brought out a book of matches and began lighting the candles.

Bakir had come to hate her gently mocking tone. He thought about telling her she could rot in hell, but decided silence was the best defiance.

'I bet you'd like me to be torn apart – by ferocious Bengali tigers, perhaps?' said Lamya, coming towards him. She stopped in front of the plinth, her small hazel eyes moving over his bruised and bloody body.

'Poor baba, you look like you've really suffered at the hands of our mistress.'

Bakir stared at her, his eyes ablaze with contempt.

'Still, you won't be the last.' Lamya traced the scabs across his chest with her fingertips. With the little strength he could muster, Bakir recoiled from the sweet itch of her touch.

'I've come to give you one final chance,' she said. 'Tell me where the Lingam is hidden. Or you die now, and we make the servant boy suffer for your obstinacy, for a very long time. We'll bring him down here and do the same to him that we've done to you. Think of it. A little boy. How much pain do you think a child can handle?'

Bakir spoke then. 'You don't have him, do you?' He thought fleetingly of how much he missed Albi, of all the effort he'd made searching for him.

Lamya laughed, but he noticed her glance down. 'Of course we have him!'

He didn't need to say any more. The glance said it all: Albi was alive and free. The brave little boy must have escaped from the Pisaca. Which meant the hiding place of the Lingam was safe – for now.

'Tell me where it is!' screeched Lamya. For a moment he caught the bitterness and frustration in her face, and inside he rejoiced.

'Why do you need it so badly?' he asked.

'Because…' began Lamya, and stopped. She thought for a moment, and then said: 'Because it can help to prevent our mistress from being drawn to the Unknown Realms, where all the Higher Ones are finally called.' She looked away, seeming to weigh something up. 'And it can help *us*, too, Baba, it can help her servants. We can use the Lingam to harness the power of the tirthas to free ourselves – partly, at least – from the chains of mortality! To know secrets others can scarcely dream of. Would you like that, Baba? I could ask my mistress if she would let you join us. There are still places left…'

Bakir went motionless for a while. Then his face began to wrinkle, and he started a parched whisper. But when the priestess eagerly leaned her ear to his mouth, he spat a mixture of blood and saliva against her cheek.

Lamya stood upright, wiping her face and fixing him with a furious look.

'I think that gives me my answer,' she said, quickly regaining her composure. She walked around the dais and he heard her open a door behind him.

'We would never have let one as pathetic as you join us, anyway,' she called, then whispered: 'Come on, my beauties...'

Bakir heard movement, accompanied by hissing and clicking. He sensed something shift in the room, and the candles seemed to burn briefly with dark flame. Then Lamya backed towards the stairs as three female creatures came in through the door.

As soon as he saw the women Bakir realised they weren't human. Besides their scabrous, jet-black skin, they had abnormally large, yellowish eyes, like cats, and their teeth were small, jagged and grey. As he watched, the tongue of the nearest slipped from her mouth and curled around in the air, like a purple worm. But what convinced him of their unnaturalness was the way he felt – *stranded*, as if all his confidence in the world had been ripped from his guts.

'I'm impressed by your loyalty to Lord Shiva. I only hope he rewards you with eternal moksha in the afterlife, once my Daginis have finished with you.' Lamya looked at the black-skinned creatures and, as she turned away, gestured casually towards the prone priest.

He had thought he was too exhausted to feel more terror, but as the creatures fell upon him with their teeth and claws, Bakir emitted one more blood-curdling scream.

*

'Damn, damn, damn, damn, damn…'

Tubs was a cool pooch but when it came to tracking he had nothing on one of those hunting beagles, Lizzie decided, as she strode back home through the woods. The little dog laboured along behind her, his straw-coloured coat bright against the snow, his breath steaming in the chilly air.

She was sure it was the feral child she'd seen, stealing food from Ashlyn's cottage. His skin was brown, like an Indian's. *Perhaps he'd come through from the Kashi tirtha.* Was it possible he'd somehow discovered the alcove at the back of the flooded room, and jumped through?

She didn't think so. He was too short, for a start. He would have struggled to climb up into the alcove. *Maybe someone had brought him through?*

She thought about that. When was the first time he'd been spotted? It was on her third day in Herefordshire, the day she'd spoken to Tom in the field. *Two days after she'd first seen Ashlyn in the garden.*

Might the intruder have brought the boy back from Kashi? *If so, why?*

Behind her Tubs sneezed and in the silence afterwards she became aware of the deep stillness of the woods. The only sound besides the dog's soft snuffling through the undergrowth was her own footsteps compressing the snow. *It was as if they were the only two creatures in the forest.*

It was really weird, to think there might be someone from India hiding in the English countryside. Had he escaped from Ashlyn? Perhaps he found everything here as strange as Lizzie found Kashi. She'd have to find him again, to see how he got here. *Perhaps he might need her help.*

Feeling frustrated, Lizzie turned her thoughts to her great-uncle's journals. How come Ashlyn had them? Had Great-Uncle Eric given them to her – or had she stolen them? Lizzie was glad she'd brought at least one with her when she started chasing the Indian child. She hoped it would fill some of the gaps in her knowledge, and help her understand the Kashi tirtha. *Perhaps it would shed some light on whether there were other tirthas in the garden.* She realised Ashlyn would know someone had been in her house and shuddered, wondering whether the witch would suspect her.

As she came back down the lane to Rowan Cottage, Lizzie saw Godwin's Range Rover parked in front of the house.

Her heart sank.

*

Inspector Faruwallah, Pandu, and Sergeant Singh were completing their circuit of the Temple of Kali when they heard the scream.

'It came from the sanctum!' shouted the Sergeant, a giant man with a brown beard, neatly pressed uniform, and white turban. He and Raj whipped out their pistols.

'Stay here!' Raj shouted to Pandu as he ran back into the inner chamber with Singh. After a moment of hesitation, Pandu ignored him and followed them through.

At the back of the sanctum the effigy of the goddess with her blade-wielding arms reared up fiercely behind the altar. A small offering of yellowed ghee lay in the bowl at her feet. The room was as quiet as before. Raj and Singh began slowly circling the edges, heading towards the statue.

The next moment another scream sounded from beneath the floor. They looked down as a different noise, a dull thumping, came from behind the Kali statue. They charged behind the effigy, and saw a trap door being pushed up by a slender arm.

Sergeant Singh knelt down and, placing his gun on the floor, yanked open the door with one hand and lifted a startled Lamya clear from the stairwell with the other. He thrust her facedown on the flagstones, and pinned her arms behind her back. Lamya gasped and cursed, and tried to kick back at him.

'You're under arrest,' he hissed, wresting his handcuffs from the holster on his belt.

But in the next moment another, even more terrifying scream came up the stairwell.

'Come on!' shouted Raj, leaping down the hole in the floor.

Singh looked urgently at Pandu. 'Can you deal with her?' he asked, passing the cuffs to the boy.

'Yes,' said Pandu, snatching them and dropping the weight of his body on to Lamya's back. The giant Sergeant seized his revolver and leapt into the hole after Raj.

But unfortunately Pandu's hold on the priestess was not as good as the Sergeant's, and she used the moment of relief to twist around like a wildcat. Before the boy knew it, she'd grabbed his wrists and was wrestling him away from her.

Pandu dropped the cuffs, amazed by the small woman's agility. He applied all his strength into breaking her grip on him, at the same time trying to use his weight to force her back on to the ground.

Down below he heard the policemen shouting, followed by a series of gunshots.

The next moment, Lamya managed to bring her knee up sharply into his stomach. Pandu's breath left him like a punctured balloon and, whilst he gasped, the priestess slipped from beneath him. With a ferocious burst of power, she hurled him against the statue of Kali, and then fled the inner sanctum and disappeared.

Pandu pushed himself up from the floor. He knew he couldn't follow her – not when his colleagues were in danger. He took a deep breath and, grasping his sore belly, stepped down into the hole in the floor.

He began to descend the dark steps.

Chapter 14:   A Battle with Daginis

'My daughter was just as difficult when she was her age.'

Rachel took the kettle off its stand and turned to face Godwin. The businessman was sitting at the kitchen table, legs crossed, crunching a biscuit.

'It's just – I feel so guilty half the time...' she said.

'You mustn't. She's got all these hormones running through her body, so the slightest thing upsets her. Sure, moving away from her friends is going to be difficult – even if she's only known them a while – but she's got to learn how to adapt. The alternative is letting her become the boss – which won't help either of you in the long run.'

'Milk?'

'Please.'

'I guess you're right,' said Rachel. 'She's so touchy about her dad. It's as if he was the perfect parent.'

'Leaving you as the bugbear? That's typical. Daisy – my first wife – was always a saint in Ginny's eyes. What happened to him – if you don't mind me asking?'

'No, that's fine. He died in an accident.'

'Oh – I'm sorry.'

'Well, you needn't be. He was supposed to be away on business – or so he told me. But everything came out after his death. He was on booked leave, and he'd gone to Scotland with his assistant. He was having an affair.'

'The cad!' said Godwin.

'Yes.'

'But Lizzie still sees him through rose-tinted spectacles?'

'Mm. She refuses to accept the facts. It's silly – I should be able to rise above it, but I can't. After all, it's her father she's lost.'

'You're only human.'

Rachel smiled. Outside, a few spots of sleet washed across the window. 'Where is she?' she said, glancing at her watch. 'She's been gone for ages. I hardly ever see her. She's either walking the dog, reading in the study, or out in the garden.'

'Really? What's she up to out there?'

'I don't know. But there's something... *unusual*... about her behaviour. It's as if she's got a secret or something. I can't quite put my finger on it.'

'I wonder what it is. Besides the moods, is anything else strange about her? Is she... tired, or anything?'

'Yes – yes she is. She's lying in late, ever since we got here.'

'I remember Ginny used to make up all these strange stories at Lizzie's age. She had three imaginary friends – a bear, a turtle, and a giant amoeba from one of Jupiter's moons! She used to wake up thinking she'd visited all these faraway places in the night.'

'Kids are so strange,' said Rachel, laughing. She gazed out of the window.

'Sounds like you need a break. I've got tickets for a play in Hay tonight. It's a comedy, an Oscar Wilde thing. It's a local am-dram group but supposed to be damned good. The person I was going with can't make it anymore. Fancy coming? We can have a meal after.'

'That sounds great – I'd love to. I so miss the theatre. Oh – there she is!' said Rachel, spotting her heavily-wrapped daughter trudging up behind Tubs on the drive.

'Shall I go?' said Godwin.

'No, please – stay and have a chat.'

*

For a few moments, the boy had frozen when he saw the girl in the house. *It was the first time he'd seen anyone there, how strange that it was the girl with the dog from the hunt.* But then he'd realised the danger he was in, and fled.

He was starting to develop a routine for survival now, despite the horrendous cold. Each morning, when the light crept in through the gaps in the cabin walls, he woke in a cold sweat from nightmares of the Pisaca. For a while he stayed swaddled in his scavenged blankets, warming his face with his breath. Finally he crawled across to his bag of provisions and ate a breakfast of something sweet if he had it, or bread otherwise, washed down with water from the stream. He rested his back against the wall, staring blankly ahead and allowing his thoughts to recover from the frazzling effects of too much cold and fear.

Once he had warmed up, he went out to search for firewood and to check whether anything had sprung the animal trap, a prize possession he'd found in one of the farmyards. He knew how to operate the trap from his time on his uncle's farm in Adabambi, where he lived and worked with his brother after his parents had died. Twice he had been lucky and found rabbits, frozen in their pain, but most often the trap was either un-sprung, or sprung but empty, a night-time denizen of the forest somewhere roaming free, unaware of how close it had come to death.

When it grew dark the boy lit a small fire with matches he'd found in the isolated cottage. Then he skinned and cooked the game, and gnawed hungrily on the greasy meat and pieces of un-rotten fruit and vegetables. Occasionally he would have something sweet to finish with – iced cakes or fried and sugared bread found in one of the large bins behind the shops. He couldn't believe what people in this cold, hellish place threw away – but it seemed somehow appropriate they should show such disrespect for good food.

The boy would then sit in front of the fire and sleep in his bedding, much more soundly than in the middle of the night when the noises of the forest were apt to wake him and fill him with dread, reminding him of his encounters with the Pisaca and her servants. At these times he felt Bakir's absence most acutely, and wept for his own miserable fate.

At some stage during the night the dying of the fire or a sharp shriek or grunt would wake him up fully and, despite his fear, he'd get up and make his way through the black trees and across the barren fields to the places where there was food, the unlit dwellings where there were no dogs or birds on guard. And he always visited the small house by the stream beyond the village, where there seemed to be an endless supply of good, fresh pickings.

But now, today, *she* had been there.

He could have lived with just being spotted – which had happened a few times before – but then she'd gone and chased him with her nasty little dog. He could hear her shouting after him through the trees in a language which, whilst he couldn't speak it as well as his brother, he knew when he heard it: English. *The language of the Empire, the language of hell.* For a while the girl and her dog had pursued him, but luckily they had been caught in undergrowth and given up.

The encounter had filled him with a fresh wave of fear. He had been close to his beloved cabin, and now wondered how safe it was. *What if the girl was a servant of the Pisaca?* Even though there'd seemed to be some kindness in her eyes, he had to assume everyone was an enemy and keep away from them. It was the only way he could hope to survive.

Reluctantly, he returned to the cabin and gathered together his things. For a while he was overwhelmed with emotion, and sat staring at the wall, tears running down his cheeks. But, despite his great setbacks, and the bitter cold, he never once considered giving up.

He left the cabin, his bag under his arm, and headed off into the bleak woods.

*

When she opened the front door Lizzie heard the sound of Godwin's voice coming from the kitchen. Still frustrated from the encounter with the wild boy, she tried to go straight into the study but her mum shouted:

'Lizzie! Come and be sociable. Godwin's here.'

Lizzie rolled her eyes. *That was the last thing she needed.* She hid the diary under the blanket in Tubs' basket and went through into the warm kitchen. Her mum and Godwin were sitting at the large pine table, drinking tea.

'Hello Lizzie,' said Godwin. 'I was just passing by and called in on the off chance.'

'Hello Mr Lennox.'

'Call me Godwin.'

'Did you have a good walk?' asked her mum.

'Yes,' said Lizzie. Her eyes began to glow as she continued: 'I saw that kid everyone's been talking about. You know, the feral kid.'

'You didn't!' said her mum.

'I did! In the woods. Tubs caught his scent.'

'Lizzie, this better not be one of your stories.'

Lizzie scowled. *Why did she even bother?*

'Are you sure it was him? What was he up to?' said Godwin.

217

'I don't know. He was hiding when Tubs saw him, in some bushes,' she lied. 'We ran after him, but he got away. We got stuck in brambles.'

'What did he look like?' asked her mum.

'He was Asian. Wearing a grey cloak, or maybe a blanket. He was young, probably only nine or ten I reckon.'

As Lizzie spoke she felt something changing in Godwin's mood. He shifted on his chair, and began to twiddle a button on the cuff of his shirt.

'Where exactly did you see him?' he asked.

'On the edge of the woods. Near the Denton road.'

'Near Limetree Cottage?'

Lizzie looked at him carefully. 'Yes.'

'All the way over there?' said her mum, raising her eyebrows. 'I thought you only took Tubs down the fields.'

'Not always.'

Lizzie glanced at Godwin and saw his eyes flick down to his mug as he drank his tea. *Something was on his mind.*

'Well, young lady, you should count yourself amongst the lucky ones,' he said. 'There's not many who can say they've seen the Wild Boy of Hebley.'

'How does he survive in this weather?' asked her mum.

'I reckon there's got to be someone helping him,' said Godwin, gulping his tea. 'I just hope it's not some pervert. There's no way a boy like that could feed himself out in the open. And he'll have had to find somewhere to keep warm too, otherwise he'd get hypothermia.'

'Maybe he's run away from a circus or something,' said her mum.

'Mum,' said Lizzie, wrinkling her nose, 'it's the twenty-first century.'

'There're still circuses,' said her mum. 'Remember the Chinese one that used to come to Hefton Park. Mr Hoo's...'

Godwin finished his tea. 'Anyway, I don't think we're going to solve the mystery of the Wild Boy right now,' he said, standing up. 'I must be on my way – I've a meeting with the A.M.M. – Agricultural Machinery Manufacturers – in Hereford. I'll see you later, Rachel,' he added, and Lizzie squirmed inside as he pecked both her mum and her on the cheek before leaving. For some reason she felt as if something had just gone horribly wrong, and wished she'd kept quiet about the boy.

'What's he mean, see you later?' she asked, as soon as Godwin had slammed the front door.

'Oh – we're going out to see a play in Hay. You don't mind, do you?' said her mum.

'No,' said Lizzie, feeling a momentary sense of dread.

*

The candlelit scene confronting Pandu at the bottom of the stairs in the Kali temple was mayhem.

The air was filled with shouting, hissing, grunting and screaming. To the left, Sergeant Singh was standing with legs apart, grappling furiously with a black-skinned, cat-like woman. At the back, below another Kali effigy, a saddhu lay tied to a stone plinth, his body covered in blood. To the right, Pandu arrived just in time to see Raj thrown to the ground by two more black-skinned women. The boy immediately recognised them from the encounter below the palace walls.

As Raj went down, his pistol flew from his hand and came spinning across the floor towards Pandu's feet. Realising the Inspector was in the most danger, Pandu snatched the surprisingly bulky gun up and ran towards the three figures struggling on the floor. One of the women had sunk her sharp teeth into Raj's shoulder, whilst the other had wrapped her taloned hands around his neck and was eagerly attempting to throttle him. Pandu had always considered himself a pacifist in

Gandhi's tradition, but he didn't hesitate to shoot as he ran forward.

The bullet launched the first creature off the Inspector and into the near wall. The other woman released Raj's shoulder from the vice-like clamp of her fangs and looked up at her new assailant. Pandu saw the silvery trickle of blood on her teeth. As she leapt at him he pulled the trigger, feeling his arm jerk again with the recoil. The woman flew backwards across the floor, and Raj scrambled to his feet, clutching his shoulder.

'Help Singh!' Pandu shouted to Raj, seeing the Sikh now pinned to the wall by his rabid foe.

'No – look!' Raj shouted, pointing back to the two that Pandu had shot. Miraculously, they were both struggling to get up from the floor.

'Here, give me the gun!' said Raj, and Pandu handed it to him. The Inspector ran to the two women and fired alternate shots into them as they tried to stand up. With each bullet they fell back, but immediately began a febrile shaking, trying to upright themselves again. Pandu saw their amber eyes roll back into their heads each time they were hit.

'Die, for the sake of Shiva!' shouted Raj as he fired. After a few moments there came a feeble clicking as the bullets finished. The two creatures lay prone, one twitching slightly like a dying fly. Whether they were dead or not, Pandu could only guess.

Pandu and the Inspector switched their attention to helping the beleaguered Sergeant. The woman's mouth was millimetres away from the man's face, her piranha teeth preparing to snap shut. Pandu saw the Sikh's eyes bulging with terror.

As the injured Raj began shakily reloading his gun, dropping every second bullet on the floor, Pandu caught sight of a poker, glowing in the embers of an iron brazier. He dived across the room and yanked it out. Then he ran up behind the woman and swiped her across the lower back.

The woman emitted a terrible caterwaul, and released the sergeant. She twisted towards Pandu, her face distorted with pain and fury. He lunged forward with the poker, causing her to back off, hissing and spitting like a cat.

Pandu advanced slowly, swinging the yellow-hot poker in front of him. The woman dodged backwards from the waist, retreating down the room.

'Through the door!' shouted Singh. Pandu glanced to his right and saw an open door behind the Kali effigy. The Sikh snatched up his revolver and began to step forward with him.

'She doesn't like the heat,' he said. 'Get her through the door and we can shut her in.'

Step by step Pandu and Singh forced the creature back, past the old man lying limp on the plinth, beneath the many wild arms of Kali, and on towards the door. All three remained locked in eye contact, ready to exploit the slightest advantage. As soon as the woman crossed the threshold of the door, Singh sprung forward and slammed it shut. He pushed the Kali effigy in front of it, jamming the handle with one of her outstretched arms.

At that moment Raj began shooting again.

Pandu and Singh turned to see that the other two women had managed to get back on their feet and cross to the Inspector, just as he was finishing reloading. He was now firing into them, but one managed to strike his chin with her clawed fist, sending him staggering back into the plinth.

'What kind of godforsaken creatures are they?' shouted Singh, as he and Pandu rushed to help. One of the women turned as she heard them, and leapt sideways like a monkey at the Sergeant.

But Singh had his own plan, and managed to reach the burning brazier before the woman got to him. As she dived forward he grabbed the iron legs of the container and launched its hot contents at her.

The creature shrieked as she was pummelled by blazing coal. Upon hearing the cry, her companion wrenched herself round, and Pandu used the chance to jump forward and strike her across the side with the poker. She screamed, and soon he had her backing away towards the door like the first one.

Then Raj was back on his feet and firing at the one whose rough skin was smouldering from the impact of the coals. With each shot, the Inspector was able to make her stagger back towards the one with Pandu, and soon he and the boy were side by side and forcing them towards the rear door. Singh meanwhile slipped behind the women whilst their attention was focused on the poker and the gun. With a quick nod at Raj and Pandu, he pulled the effigy away and flung the door open. He leapt out of the way, enabling the Inspector and boy to force the women back the final few steps across the threshold. Then the burly Sergeant sprang forward and slammed the door. He remained with his back against it, sweating and looking at Pandu and Raj. After a moment, they all grinned with relief.

'What on earth are they?' said Raj, panting and gripping his shoulder.

Suddenly a groan came from the table. They looked round at the bloody figure of the old man, who Pandu had assumed was dead. The bearded head rocked slightly.

Whilst Singh held the door, Pandu and Raj approached the priest. His wrists and ankles were bound with leather cord, and his frail body was a patchwork of scabs, cuts, and bruises. Around his torso and limbs he was stitched with neat puncture wounds, as if he'd been savaged by small sharks. But his eyes were open, blinking at them weakly.

'Those – *things* – were actually eating him when we arrived,' whispered Raj.

'It's him!' exclaimed Pandu. 'The old man from the Lakshmi Temple!' It had taken him a moment to recognise the injured priest.

The old man made another sound, and they leaned close to hear what he was trying to say.

'I – recognise you now,' he said, looking at Pandu. 'You are – his brother…'

'What? Albi – my brother?' said Pandu.

'Yes – Albi…' Bakir burst into a fit of coughing, and more blood trickled from the side of his mouth. 'I saw you once at the Blue Temple.'

'Quick – cut the ropes!' said Raj, grabbing a pair of curved ceremonial knives from the table where the blood-stained torture equipment was neatly laid out. Pandu helped the Inspector sever the cords, and Raj slipped his arm under the old man's back to lift him slightly. Bakir's coughing eased, but his breathing remained laboured. After a moment he began to whisper again:

'I think he's still – alive. I looked in all the morgues – but never found him. There's hope. I'm sure he would be here – if they had him…'

'My brother is alive?' repeated Pandu. 'How do you know?'

The old man's head dipped. '*May* be alive,' he gasped. His eyelids quivered for a moment, and it looked like he was slipping away. Raj pulled out his handkerchief and dabbed the priest's sweaty brow.

'Stay with us, baba,' he said. 'Singh! Call an ambulance!'

The Sergeant already had his radio in his hand. 'I'm not getting a signal,' he said.

'No point, anyway,' said Bakir. 'I'm not going to make it – seen too much. But Albi knows where it is – that's why they want him…'

'Where what is?' asked Raj.

'The – Lingam. It – *hurts* her – badly. We saw it burn her. But she needs it – to escape – the Unknown Realms. And *they* need it too! They want to – *corrupt* – nature. But…' – Pandu was sure the hint of a smile played on the old man's lips, 'we hid it from her…'

'Who are you talking about?' said Raj. 'Who tried to steal the Lingam?'

'The – *Pisaca*...' Bakir whispered, and they were the last words he said.

Chapter 15: Hunted by Dogs

Albi was trudging through the snowy undergrowth at the edge of the wood when he heard the huntsman's horn.

In a rush of alarm, he turned and scanned the broad fields stretching back towards the village. He spotted half a dozen riders, chasing recklessly on the heels of a pack of dogs in his direction. Next moment the muffled sound of the dogs' yelping came across the snow-padded land.

Clutching his bag of provisions tight under his arm, Albi ran into the cover of the trees. He went far enough to ensure he couldn't be seen from the fields, but not so far that he lost sight of the hunters. He ran for a while like that, jumping through bracken and between tree trunks before he realised – as he'd feared – that the riders weren't changing direction.

He decided to head deeper into the woods, to hide within the tangle of trees and undergrowth.

He ran hard and fast for a while, before he finally had to stop beside an icy stream, gasping for breath and sweating. He grabbed a mossy trunk to steady himself, and fought back an urge to be sick. He'd only run like that once before, fleeing the Pisaca with Bakir.

After regaining his breath, Albi held up his head and listened. All he could hear was the brook beside him, splashing and gurgling between snow-capped stones. A tiny brown bird darted across the stream into a messy heap of prickly green leaves and red berries. Albi watched the bird hop about, deep in the shadow of the bush.

The next moment the peace was destroyed by the yapping of the dogs, and the thrashing noise as they forced their way through bracken and brambles. Albi felt a sharp coldness inside. This time they weren't hunting a fox. *They were hunting him.*

He'd thought he had no more energy, but next he was splashing through the brook, barely noticing the icy water, and fleeing again through the gloomy forest. He bashed his shin against a tree root, but kept on running.

Behind, he heard the dogs catching on him, and caught the dull thud of hooves pummelling the ground. At least two riders were with them. Briefly he wondered if they would just run him down and kill him. Maybe they no longer cared about the Lingam. Or perhaps they'd found Bakir and made him tell them where it was. He forced from his mind a premonition of the dogs leaping on top of him and tearing at his flesh.

The dogs and riders continued to gain on him. He began to feel a deep, physical dread overtaking him. He could *never* outrun them. He was going to have to give in, he couldn't keep going forever. The din behind was so terrible, he imagined that the lead dogs would be snapping at his heels any moment. But when he glanced back they were further away than he'd thought. He saw the hounds leap a fallen tree, followed by a demon Raksasa on horseback, his framed eyes burning with unholy flame. Behind him was another Raksasa, just a dark shape in the saddle.

Albi knew there was still no hope. There was nowhere to hide; it was only a matter of time before they caught him. With tears streaming down his cheeks, he sensed the cruel irony of his fate – to have survived so long, in the rain and cold and snow, only to be killed like this, lost and alone in hell...

And then he glanced the other way, and caught a streak of russet coat and crimson-tipped tail coming through the trees towards him.

The fox! He watched as it weaved swiftly, effortlessly between the forest's jumble of trunks, thorns and stems. The creature stopped a few paces in front of him, looking up with clear hazel eyes. For a moment boy and fox regarded each other intensely.

Then the fox flicked its head to the left, twice in succession. Albi followed its glance and spotted a giant oak tree, its ancient trunk split in two by lightning and age. Without even thinking, he ducked down into the undergrowth and scrambled into the dark heart of the tree.

When he peeked back out, struggling to keep the noise of his breathing down, he was amazed to see the fox jumping calmly through the snow *towards* the dogs. When the beagles spotted it, their yapping rose a pitch. They set off straight for the fox, as it changed its course and fled away through the trees.

And so the dogs, followed by the blissfully unaware riders, disappeared into the dank, grey woods, chasing his mysterious saviour. Albi shrank back into the deep, musty recess of the oak, no longer daring to look out.

Slowly, the barking of the dogs and the crashing of the horses faded, and the woods grew quiet. Albi felt the hammering of his heart subside, and his breathing returned to normal. He stared at the ground and began counting backward from one hundred, as his brother had taught him to do whenever he was scared.

After a moment, he heard a faint rustle, and noticed a dimming of the light on the soil around his feet. He frowned, and looked up.

Albi screamed, cowering back from the tall, hooded woman with the fierce green eyes...

*

As soon as Godwin had left, Lizzie hurried out into the increasingly gloomy garden with Tubs. Whilst she knew she had to devise a plan to find the wild boy, she was itching to find out if there were more tirthas. But first she ran to the Indian garden and checked to see whether the cotton was gone.

It was, which meant Ashlyn must be back. Lizzie marvelled for a moment at the witch's bare-faced cheek, stealing her great-uncle's diaries *and* sneaking about through her garden. She realised Ashlyn must head out through another area during the day, perhaps somewhere in the Pond garden where there wasn't a proper hedge or fence and you could push through the undergrowth into the woods. *Unbelievable!*

Then she ran back to the Gothic garden, and crossed the snowy lawn to the small statue of a monk.

'Is this one of them?' she said, looking down at Tubs. The little dog stared blankly up at her, flecks of snow melting on his whiskers.

'You know, sometimes I think you know more than you're letting on – and other times I just think you're daft,' she muttered. She reached forward to grab the man's head – and stopped. What if it *was* a tirtha? Where might it transport her?

'I don't know if I should...' she said.

'Should what?' It was her mum, standing behind her in the entrance to the garden.

'Mum! You made me jump!'

'Sorry,' said her mum, rubbing her sides. She was wearing her red anorak and her black woolly hat pulled down to her eyebrows. Ambling across the lawn, she added: 'I just put your clothes in the wash. They were filthy. What have you been doing?'

'Nothing.'

Her mum turned and looked around the borders. 'You're spending a lot of time out here,' she said.

'Am I?' said Lizzie, casually.

'Yes. You are,' said her mum. She looked at Lizzie. 'You got a cold?'

'No.'

'Godwin pointed out how red you look. Have you got windburn or something?'

Lizzie's face did feel a bit sore and tight. Suddenly she realised what it was - sunburn! There was an

233

elongated silence as she found herself lost for words, then her mum said:

'Look at that little statue.'

Tubs stood knee-deep in the snow, watching Lizzie's mum expectantly with his mouth open. His tongue was bubblegum pink.

Lizzie glanced round. 'Oh yeah,' she said, as if it was the first time she'd seen it. She began to feel uncomfortable.

'I met old Mr Barrow in the village yesterday. He told me you were talking to him about the garden, at Eva's party. He said you were keen to know about the cottage's previous owner, Eric's mother, Evelyn.'

Lizzie frowned. 'I only wanted to know who made the garden.'

Her mum turned and fixed her with one of her stares, before adding: 'I don't want you hiding things from me, Lizzie Jones. You got me?'

Lizzie didn't reply.

'Look, Lizzie. I know it's all a strain in this new place. But remember – you can still talk to me about things. I am your mother.'

Lizzie nodded sheepishly.

'Anyway. It's freezing out here. I'm going back in.'

As soon as she heard her mum slam the door back into the house, Lizzie reached out and grabbed the tonsured head of the statue. She took a deep breath, and began to circle it slowly. After several circuits she stopped and pushed the statue back until the base came out of the soil and the head touched the pine tree behind. Nothing happened. She set it back upright, and leapfrogged over it, catching herself against the tree. *Nothing.* She began to feel silly, and looked back at Tubs.

'Ain't gonna work, is it?' she said.

The dog tilted his head quizzically.

Chapter 16:   The Temple of Ganesh

Pandu woke from a deep, dreamless slumber to a dull vibration in his ear.

Quickly, he pulled his phone out from under the pillow, fearing the buzzing would wake the other boys snoring and coughing around him in the dark dormitory. He opened the text and read:

Out of hospital. Meet you at compound in 30 mins. R.

He yawned deeply, rubbed his eyes, and checked the time on the phone. 10:15pm – he'd been asleep for five hours, exhausted from the encounter in the temple. Beside him, Daljit Narlikar murmured in his sleep. As quietly as he could, Pandu climbed out of bed and looked out of the skylight across the city. From his vantage point high in the rafters of the former Institute for Social Reform, Science and Literature, he could see a trio of rickshaw drivers in the streetlights below, waiting for tourists from the upmarket Hotel Plaza. Cars swept past, tooting their horns.

His brother might still be alive!

A shudder of excitement ran down Pandu's spine. He hardly dared believe it, in case it turned out not to be true. But, before he'd died, the old priest said he thought Albi lived. And if so, the big question was: *where?*

Before the old priest died... The horror of that underground chamber swept over him again. He closed his eyes and focused his mind on the holy area, the area of eternal light, just behind his brow. He prayed for the priest's soul, that it had suffered enough, and should never again have to go through the pain of rebirth. After that, he prayed one more time that he would see his little brother again.

When he'd finished his prayers, he pulled on his shirt and trousers and slipped his phone into his pocket. Then he picked up his dusty flip flops, intending to put them on outside so he could leave as quietly as possible. He had a lot to do, and didn't want to spend hours answering questions from the other boys as he had earlier in the afternoon. Beside him, Daljit muttered something else in his sleep, his sheet as usual all but discarded. The stocky boy was a heavy sleeper and unlikely to wake, but there were other lighter sleepers who started to yawn, cough and peel their eyes open as Pandu crept over the creaking floorboards towards the stairs.

'Pandu – is it true what they said about you? That you saw a saddhu *murdered* in the Kali temple?' asked little Saleem Mustapha in his oddly-pitched, soon-to-be-truly-broken voice, as Pandu tried to tiptoe past his bed. Saleem served at the Banaras Gentleman's Club, and had only got back to the dorm after Pandu had finished telling his story.

'Go back to sleep, Saleem,' he hissed.

'But Pandu –'

Before the small boy could ask any more questions, Pandu jumped away down the stairs.

The Institute for Social Reform, Science and Literature was a huge colonial edifice, built during the British Empire in India. It had long since ceased to be used for its original purpose, proudly inscribed above the main entrance: *The progressive improvement of the educational attainment amongst poor and promising children'*. Now it housed a multitude of activities and organizations, including the headquarters of a mail order company, a school for modern Indian dance, and a print room for the Municipality of Varanasi. Ownership of the building had passed from a charitable trust set up by a business tycoon to the Municipality, which now ran it on a shoestring budget, meaning that paint flaked, floorboards rotted, and windows accumulated layer upon layer of dust and traffic soot. But the one good thing the Municipality had done was to keep the rooms at the top for homeless children without families. Pandu had been living there for three years. Like him, many of the orphans worked in the city's temples or public buildings, although it wasn't unusual for some of the more wayward to turn to gangs and begging.

When he left the Institute, Pandu headed towards the temple of Ganesh in Vishwanatha. As usual, he diverted briefly down to the river, where he knelt at the lowest ghat and splashed cold water over his face. He glanced across the dark Ganges and said a short prayer to Shiva, then hurried around the back of the temple to the pound where Ramses was kept.

The God Ganesh was the son of Parvati, who was the wife of Shiva. Legend held that Ganesh had been beheaded by Shiva in a fit of jealous anger, when he found the boy guarding his wife as she bathed. Parvati insisted that Shiva heal Ganesh, so he stormed off, intending to take the head of the first creature he came across to replace the boy's. It turned out to be an elephant, and now all elephants were sacred to Ganesh. And thus Vishram, the presiding priest at the temple, had ruled that one be kept permanently for holy ceremonies. It was Pandu's job to take care of Ramses, which he'd been doing for two years.

Ramses had been donated as a calf to the temple by an outlying elephant farm. He was now thirteen years old, almost fully grown by elephant standards. Every day, Pandu cleaned and fed him, and exercised him with a walk along the ghat.

'How are you tonight, my Scourge of Demons?' he said, as he entered the compound and saw Ramses' monolithic form standing in the darkness. Pandu flicked on the outside light, and the elephant snorted and lifted his great trunk at him. He tried to dab Pandu's forehead as the boy approached.

'Leave off!' said Pandu, laughing and pushing the trunk away. Ramses let his trunk fall, then sprung it up again, forcing Pandu to catch it and give it a vigorous rubbing. The elephant sidled sideways a little, relishing the physical contact.

'You're hungry, aren't you? Sorry I've been so long – but you wouldn't believe what's happened. Albi might still be alive!' Pandu strode over and grabbed an armful of hay from the feeding tray which the elephant, chained to a heavy post, couldn't reach. He brought it over and Ramses stuffed it greedily into his maw with his trunk. Pandu gathered several more armfuls and dropped them down before the elephant. Then, as the great beast gorged happily on its evening meal, the boy walked around him, scrubbing his feet and hide with a brush dipped in a pail of water.

Pandu loved this ritual because it gave him time to think, something he rarely had time to do during the hot busy day. He often talked to the elephant as it munched down its hay. But now he worked in silence, his thoughts churning with images of the saddhu and the women, but above all with the hope that *his brother might still be alive…*

As he scrubbed the elephant's leathery flank, a screech came from the gate hinges. He spun round to see Inspector Faruwallah standing there in his uniform, his arm neatly bandaged and held in a white sling.

'How are you, Uncle?' said Pandu, drawing back from the elephant. Whilst Raj wasn't his real uncle, Pandu used the familiar term when they weren't in public.

'OK,' said Raj, striding over to Ramses and rubbing the elephant's forehead. Ramses' soft eyelashes blinked a couple of times, but he didn't look up from the food.

'How's the shoulder?'

'Sore as hell. The doctor said it was going septic quicker than anything he'd ever seen before. He had to give me an almighty jab of tetanus – like being kicked in the butt by a donkey! That, on top of twenty stitches.'

'And still they let you come back to work?'

'Well no, not officially. They told me to take the week off. But there're important things to do.'

'Did you tell them about how those creatures wouldn't die?'

'No. What's the point? No one would ever believe it. I think that's between you, me and Singh for the while. We're OK with Singh, he's one of the best men I've got. We can trust him.'

'Did the reinforcements find any trace of them?' asked Pandu.

'No.'

Pandu, Raj and Singh had stayed in the chamber with the body of the priest until the police backup and ambulance arrived. During their wait, they scraped the coals back into the brazier and reheated the poker. The other policemen threw each other strange looks as their boss insisted they prepare to shoot to kill 'unarmed but deadly' women trapped behind the rear door, and then stood ready with a poker in his good hand. But when Sergeant Singh swung the door open the room beyond was empty. Searching around, one of the officers discovered a grate in the floor which opened into a sewage tunnel. Several policemen, along with Pandu,

Raj, and Singh, dropped down into the tunnel and followed it by torchlight as it sloped gently upwards for several hundred metres. Finally, they spotted daylight ahead and discovered an open manhole in the roof. Hoisted up on the shoulders of Singh, Pandu recognised the street by the palace, where he and Lizzie had first encountered the strange women.

'What about the priestess?' asked Pandu. 'Did they catch her?' He had got down on his knees, and was finishing off the elephant's lumpy nails with a small brush.

'No,' said Raj. 'We've closed the temple and put a warrant out for her arrest. We're doing our best now to control the press. I don't know what the headlines will be like tomorrow, but dread to think. Can you imagine? We only need one medic saying something about torture and cannibalism in the Kali temple and, what with the Pisaca and the Lingam, we'll have a mass panic on our hands.'

'But maybe that could help the investigation? Lots of people on the lookout...'

'It's too much for the average man on the street,' said Raj. 'People already know about the Pisaca and the child murders. Let them guess about the closure of the temple.'

'Do you think any of those black-skinned…
creatures… are the Pisaca?' asked Pandu. 'Or maybe the
Pisaca is the priestess, Lamya?'

'Or all of them together,' said Raj, shrugging. 'Who
knows? But none of them match the descriptions we've
had so far. That woman you and the English girl
followed seems more likely.'

'I'm sure everything must be connected,' said Pandu.
He finished brushing the last of Ramses' toes.

'Come on,' said the Inspector. 'We must get to this
temple and check it out – see if it gives us any clues
about this strange English girl.'

'So many mysteries…' said Pandu, grasping Ramses'
flapping ear. 'See you in the morning,' he whispered.

As they left the compound, the elephant trumpeted
its annoyance at not coming too.

Chapter 17:   A Visitor at Night

'Godwin and I are going for a meal after the play, so I'll be back late – don't wait up!'

Standing in the hallway, Lizzie tilted her head back for her mum to kiss her goodbye.

'Lizzie – don't look so glum! He's only a *friend*.'

Lizzie listened as the big Range Rover reversed out of the drive, crunching gravel. In the oppressive silence that followed, she thought about her dad and felt close to tears. Then her leg was nudged and she looked round to see Mr Tubs staring up at her, his brown eyes full of softness.

She knelt down, and hugged him against her.

'What would I do without you, boy?' she asked, and received a barrage of wet tongue against her nose and forehead.

'There'd be a lot less slobber to deal with...'

She considered her plan for the evening. She'd been thinking about searching the garden to see if she could find another tirtha – but now she didn't feel like traipsing about in the cold. She decided instead to make a fire in the study, and read her great-uncle's diary. With any luck she'd find out what he did in Kashi – and perhaps discover how the other tirthas worked. And then she'd try and work out what to do about the wild boy.

'Come on, Mr Tubs,' she said. 'Let's go get some wood.'

Once the fire was lit and the dog had settled down on the rug, she sat down in the armchair with the journal on her lap. She flicked through the pages, and saw it was dated from 1999 to 2001. She began to read the first page:

17th July 1999.

Delphiniums in full bloom. This is their best year yet, their soft, sky-blue flowers a delight, blending harmoniously with the pinks of the roses. The weather this morning was glorious, and as I stood up from a bout of weeding in the Master-of-Nets, I couldn't help but marvel at my fortune. Why should I, of all this Earth's countless millions, be so lucky as to reside in this miraculous place?

The Master-of-Nets – that was one of the gardens, with the tiny oriental-looking houses and ornaments. The journal contained references to other rooms in the garden, but it didn't take her long to find her first reference to Kashi:

25th February 2000.

Spent a few pleasant hours visiting the Jantar Mantar observatory near Dashashwamedha ghat. The instruments, built in the eighteenth century by Jai Singh, Maharajah of Jaipur, are small, but many are still accurate, and the equatorial sundial is a pleasure.

Afterwards I met Bakir at our usual spot in the Lakshmi temple. He took me around some other places in the city I hadn't seen, such as the Alamgir Mosque and the Durga temple, overrun with cheeky, pink-faced monkeys – one of which managed to pinch my lassi drink. The little blighter bounced away with it down the street, spraying a group of children with the yoghurt as he passed.

We ended up back at the Blue Temple, where Bakir was able to persuade the Hindu priests to give me a privileged viewing of the inner sanctum. There I was able to admire the sacred stone Lingam, one of the holiest artefacts of Shiva...'

Lizzie looked up at Tubs, quivering in his sleep by the fire. She marvelled, thinking how both she and her great-uncle had shared such an incredible experience.

But... did *he* ever encounter the Pisaca?

*

A few people were still milling about on the shadowy ghats near the river's edge when Pandu and Inspector Faruwallah reached the temple at the end of Dashashwamedha ghat. A man was doing his puja, stooped at the edge of the black water, and a seated priest was preparing marigold necklaces for the next day's trade.

'This is one of the oldest temples in the city,' said Raj. 'I know it. It was a Brahma temple, but it's not been used for decades. Even when I was a boy it was derelict.'

Pandu supported the Inspector's injured arm as the portly man stepped up on to the ledge. They then shuffled out over the water and around to the small, covered archway, with its concealed flight of steps.

'She went down there,' said Pandu, pointing into the pitch black.

As instructed, Raj had brought police torches. He handed one to Pandu, then switched his on and began to descend the steep stairway.

At the bottom, Pandu stood on the stairs behind Raj as the Inspector flashed his torch around the warm, humid chamber. The beam lit up the black dripping walls, streaked with green mould. Directing the light over the water, they spotted some broken pieces of stone or rock.

'By Krishna!' Raj exclaimed.

'Well, go on, then!' said Pandu.

Raj nodded and took a tentative step forward into the water. A couple of loose stones shifted under his foot before it came to rest on the floor. The cold water seeped into his shoe and through his sock.

'Yuck!' he said.

Pandu stepped around the Inspector into the shallow water and shone his torch at a low stone construction in the corner. 'A kund,' he said, going and pointing the beam down the well. A small glint in the blackness at the bottom suggested more water. Then he noticed an alcove halfway up the wall at the back of room, and made his way over to it. He shone the light in.

'Look, Uncle – an effigy!'

Raj waded over and peered into the hole. The stone at the back had been carved into a crude, semi-circular form with several heads, each facing different directions. Beside the heads was a squat bird with a cartoonish face and beak.

'Four heads symbolising Brahma, the all-seeing and all-knowing. And look, there's his steed, the sacred goose,' he said.

Pandu reached back and pushed the carving with his hand. 'Nothing giving,' he said. 'There must be some other way out.'

'Where has all this rubble come from?' asked Raj, feeling something crack under his heel as he stepped forwards. He knelt down and, sliding the torch into his sling, used his good hand to lift a large round piece of rock out of the water.

Pandu looked up warily. 'Maybe the ceiling caving in?'

'Oh my God…'

Pandu turned to the Inspector, who was staring in horror at the thing in his hands.

'It's a skull – a *child's* skull!'

*

A sudden banging woke Lizzie from her slumber. She sat up and looked round, taking a moment to remember where she was.

The study. Her great-uncle's study, with the two lamps on, and the fire crackling in the hearth. She had fallen asleep reading. Quickly, she lifted the open journal off her belly, and placed it on the small table beside her. She checked the clock above the mantelpiece: 8.10.

Who was banging?

Feeling a pang of anxiety, she looked round for Tubs. He'd been making muffled half-barks, dreaming in front of the fire, before she fell asleep. Now the study door had opened a crack. *He must be in the hall.*

Suddenly there was another loud bang, followed by a bout of snarling. He *was* in the hall.

What should she do?

When she was home alone in her gran's flat in Croydon Lizzie never answered the door to anyone, unless she knew it was one of her friends. It wasn't because she was scared to, it was just that it was almost certain to be a door-to-door salesman, trying to flog you a better gas deal or a new kitchen.

But who would knock on your door at night, in the middle of the countryside?

Tubs began to bark.

What should she do?

She stood up and peered round the doorframe into the hall. The little dog had his chin pressed right up against the door, and was yapping his head off. Whoever was outside would know - *or at least suspect -* someone was in, from the lights on in the hall and kitchen. Lizzie was afraid to move into the hall, in case they could see her through the little oblong window beside the door. An image of Ashlyn standing in her cloak in the snow outside flashed through her mind.

Had the child killer finally got wise to her? Was she here to get her?

Suddenly Tubs stopped barking.

Lizzie held her breath, straining to hear what the caller was doing. She thought she could make out the crunching of gravel, and prayed that whoever it was, was heading away up the drive. Everything went quiet.

'Come here, Tubs,' she whispered, crouching down and holding out her arms.

But just as the dog started trotting towards her, she heard a dull thudding.

The visitor was coming down the path beside the kitchen!

Heart thumping, Lizzie twisted round and shrieked as a large white face pressed up against the latticed window of the study.

And then let out a sigh of relief, as she realised it was Eva.

'Lizzie – it's only me – sorry to scare you!' the tall woman shouted through the window.

'It's OK,' said Lizzie, standing up. 'I'll let you in!'

But Tubs began to bark again, and Lizzie only just managed to catch him as he launched himself across the room. Quickly, she thrust him back into the hall and slammed the door on him. Then, ignoring his muffled growling, she went over to the door and unlocked it.

'I was just passing by and wondered if you fancied another ride tomorrow?' said Eva, smiling.

Lizzie nodded. 'Yes, please,' she said. 'I really enjoyed our last one.'

'Me too,' said Eva. 'It's nice to have company.'

She stood awkwardly at the threshold for a moment until Lizzie realised she should ask her in.

'Would you like some tea?' she said.

'That would be great. It's freezing out!'

'Come in,' said Lizzie.

Eva stepped into the room and wiped her feet on the small mat. She was wearing a long dark winter coat, which she began to unbutton. Lizzie shut the door behind her.

'Sorry I didn't answer,' she said. 'But I'm on my own tonight.'

'Oh really – where's your mum?'

'She's gone to see a play.'

Eva nodded. Outside the door, Tubs began to bark.

'Would you like to sit down?' said Lizzie, gesturing to the armchair in front of the fire. 'I'll put the kettle on.'

She had to be quick to shove Tubs back as she opened the door into the hall. She dragged him back into the lounge and then, when he continued to bark, further on into the kitchen. She slammed the door and, before even turning the light on, squatted down beside him.

'What's got into you?' she hissed. 'Behave!'

Kneeling down, she didn't notice as two figures – one tall, the other short – stole quickly past the window…

*

'By Krishna, I swear there's no other way out of this godforsaken pit!'

Pandu watched as Raj sat down on one of the lower steps, dabbing his brow with a pristine white handkerchief. The boy knew how fastidious the Inspector was, and could see he was increasingly irritated by wading through the water with his shoes and socks soaked.

They had checked the walls and stairs – trying not to disturb the bones – but found nothing. It was beginning to look like a hopeless task.

Pandu went and sat down beside the Inspector.

'You're absolutely sure this was where she came?' Raj asked, for the third time.

Pandu nodded, frowning. 'I don't understand,' he said. 'It just doesn't make sense.'

'I think it's time to give up,' said the Inspector. 'The crime scene unit can make another check – when they arrive.' He checked his watch. 'Late as usual,' he muttered.

The torch they'd placed on the edge of the well fluttered for a moment as its battery began to fade. Shadows flittered on the glistening, green-stained walls.

'OK, let's go outside,' said Raj, standing up. 'I'll get the torch.'

He stood up and waded across the room, through the crushed bones and water. Suddenly he shouted:

'Pandu – look!'

Pandu, who was starting to climb the stairs, looked back into the room to where the Inspector was pointing the torch. As he watched, his jaw went slack and fell open.

For, at the back of the chamber, in the alcove with the ancient engraving of Brahma, it seemed as if the solid stone was disappearing into a mass of folding darkness. Pandu shook his head, unable to believe his eyes. He remembered his science lessons, and wondered for a second whether he was witnessing something incredible, like the appearance of a black hole.

And then he realised – equally unbelievably, he knew – that it was a *person* taking shape before him, wrapped in a black cloak. And he frowned, because he was sure that they'd checked, and checked again – and there was no secret opening at the back of that hole...

Chapter 18:   The Fight on the Ghat

'You're not a wolf!' said Lizzie, angrily shutting Tubs in the kitchen and heading back through the house with a pot of tea on a tray, laid out like her gran would do it, with a pink cosy over the pot.

As she opened the study door Eva looked up from the armchair, where she was reading Lizzie's great-uncle's diary.

'Sorry – I was being nosy,' said the woman, blushing.

'It's OK,' said Lizzie, turning away to mask a sudden sense of discomfort. Her great-uncle's diary was special, *for her alone.* She put the tray down on the desk instead of the table, concealing her expression from Eva.

'Lizzie, I'm sorry, really,' said Eva. 'It's very rude of me.'

Lizzie turned back, and glanced into Eva's eyes. 'Don't worry – honestly,' she said. 'How do you like your tea?'

'Just a splash of milk.'

As she passed Eva the cup Lizzie noticed her hand was still wrapped in a bandage.

'Does that still hurt?' she said, spotting a small pink welt on Eva's other hand too.

'Yes,' said Eva. 'I went to the doctor this morning and she gave me some antibiotics. She thinks it's infected.'

Lizzie frowned in sympathy, and pulled the chair out from the desk. She sat down opposite Eva in front of the fire. They talked for a while about the horses, and she soon began to feel happy and relaxed again.

'If you want, you can come riding more regularly,' said Eva. 'The farmer's daughter's got a new job in Hereford, and someone's going to have to give Isobel some exercise.'

'That would be great,' said Lizzie.

'Good.'

They sat for a moment in silence, both staring at the fire. Then Eva said:

'Lizzie – you know how, when we were riding the other day, you asked me whether I'd ever been to India?'

Lizzie felt a surge of anxiety, and threw Eva a sidelong glance. 'Uh – yeah,' she said.

'Were you interested because of your great-uncle's diary? He certainly seems to have spent a lot of time over there.'

'Yes, I suppose,' said Lizzie, finding it hard to look Eva in the eye.

'From what I've just read, it seems like he went back and forward to Kashi like a yo-yo.'

She knew something! Lizzie was sure of it. She glanced up into Eva's eyes, which were studying her calmly. *What should she do?* Was Eva giving her the chance to say something? *What did she know?*

'Lizzie – if there's anything you'd like to say to me – *anything* – you know you can trust me.'

Lizzie looked up. *She was desperate to tell someone.* Drawing in a deep breath, she said:

'You know, don't you?'

Eva gave a slight nod.

'How?'

'Your great-uncle told me everything before he died. He wanted me to help him explore the tirthas. But he was worried.'

'Why?'

'Because of Ashlyn Williams, and the other witches.'

Lizzie stared at her dumbfounded.

'He thought Ashlyn might have read his diary,' Eva continued, 'and begun using the tirthas too. And worse, he thought she'd made some kind of pact with the Kali cult in Kashi – a pact that involved terrible sacrifices to gain special powers.' She paused, fixing Lizzie with a determined stare, then added gravely: 'Lizzie – these sacrifices – they were *child* sacrifices.'

Lizzie was scarcely able to believe what she was hearing. *Eva knew so much.* After a moment she said: 'So – you know about the Pisaca, too?'

'Yes. I'm sure Ashlyn *is* the Pisaca.'

'We thought so, too!'

'We?'

'Yes – me and Pandu.'

'Who's Pandu?'

'He's a temple boy from Kashi. He's been helping the police search for the Pisaca because he thinks she captured his brother.'

'Why would she have done that?'

'I don't know,' Lizzie wrinkled her nose. 'Probably to sacrifice him or something.'

'Oh God.'

'Yes,' said Lizzie, frowning. 'But me and Pandu are going to try and catch her – with the help of the Indian police. I've seen her going through the garden to the tirtha –' Lizzie glanced at Eva again '– and I followed her last night, with Pandu, and he heard her talking to this crazy old priest in the Lakshmi temple. The priest was saying something about how he'd hidden this *Lingam* thing, a sort of holy relic, from the Pisaca, because she wanted it for some reason, we don't know why, but he said it could hurt her…'

'Woah, Lizzie!' said Eva. 'You're going much too fast. What is this *Lingam*?'

'It's a sort of special stone, a holy stone of Shiva, and it's normally kept in the Blue Temple where Pandu's brother used to work, and people think it protects the city but it was stolen a while ago and now everyone thinks that's why the city is being attacked by the Pisaca.'

'It's all kind of… *supernatural*, isn't it?' said Eva. 'Do you believe in any of that stuff?'

'I don't know,' said Lizzie, pausing to think. 'But I broke into Ashlyn's cottage the other day and found she'd stolen my great-uncle's diaries and I read a bit of them, and *he* thinks there's some connection between the tirtha – or *tirthas* – and this kind of *plane* that they're all on, where maybe gods and mythical creatures actually *live*… Which sounds mad, totally mad, but then I was attacked in Kashi by these women with horrible teeth and black skin who were naked and really weird and I could just… *feel* they weren't human. Can you believe that?'

As soon as she stopped for breath, Lizzie began to feel giddy. She'd been looking down at the rug as she talked, and now the room suddenly felt very warm. *And there was still so much more to tell.* She looked up at Eva imploringly.

'You've experienced so much,' said Eva. 'It's hard to take in all you're saying. Take a deep breath, and have a drink.'

Lizzie did as she was told, and began to feel a bit better. Immediately another thought occurred to her. 'Have you been through, then, Eva?'

'Through the tirtha to Kashi?'

Lizzie nodded.

'Yes. Just a couple of times – briefly. But look, before I tell you about that, tell me everything you know about this Lingam. It sounds to me as if it might hold the key to the whole mystery of what Ashlyn – *the Pisaca* – is up to.'

Lizzie nodded enthusiastically, and looked up at the clock on the mantelpiece. Eva glanced at it too, and said: 'When are your mum and Godwin back?'

'Not 'til late,' said Lizzie. 'They've gone to see...' Suddenly she stopped.

Eva looked at her and smiled.

'Lizzie – are you sure you're OK?' she said.

'Yes,' said Lizzie. 'I just feel a bit woozy again. Perhaps I'd better go and get a glass of water.'

'Shall I come with you?'

'No – no. I'll only be a minute.'

Eva smiled again. 'Sure,' she said.

*

As the black shape continued to solidify miraculously in the alcove, Pandu charged across the room and pushed Raj's torch down.

'Quick Uncle!' he whispered, 'Hide!'

'Wha…' began the Inspector, but then his instincts took over and he crouched down behind the well with the boy, stifling a cry as his shoulder jarred. He switched off the torch.

In darkness, they held their breath and waited.

After a moment, they heard a loud splash and cracking sound, as someone dropped down from the alcove into the water. But then, instead of the anticipated noise of the person crossing the chamber, there was another long pause. Pandu shut his eyes tightly, praying he and Raj hadn't been heard. He pictured the Pisaca standing there, her wolfish eyes peering through the darkness.

And then a low woman's voice said: 'Come on…'

There was another splash, which Pandu thought must be a *second* person coming into the chamber. *Where were they coming from?*

Next there was the sound of crunching as the two made their way through the waterlogged room. As they approached the antechamber Pandu's eyes, growing accustomed to the darkness, could make out one tall shape – *surely the Pisaca* – walking alongside a smaller, childlike form. And then they were gone, away up the steps.

'Who was that?' hissed Raj, bumping Pandu as he stood up and turned on his torch.

'It's the Pisaca. Maybe she really is a demon, coming out of thin air like that...' said Pandu. Then he added: 'Come on, Uncle – we have to follow her!'

The two ran back through the chamber and looked up. The Pisaca and her companion had disappeared, so they bounded up the steps. Just before the exit, Pandu crouched down and peered around the corner.

'It's clear,' he said, shuffling on to the moonlit ledge and heading towards the main part of the city. He needed to get to the corner quickly to see where they were going. But as he moved, he glanced back and saw the Inspector struggling on the ledge due to his injured arm. Pandu's face dropped. He didn't want to lose the Pisaca – but if he slowed to help Raj he was sure to.

The Inspector, sweating with the effort of trying to move quickly, stopped. A look of understanding passed between them.

'Go on,' said Raj. 'Follow them. But keep a distance, and don't do anything dangerous. *At all.* I'll call for backup now. You've got your phone – keep me informed where they go and I'll be with you as soon as I can.'

Pleased to be trusted, Pandu nodded and smiled. He turned and shuffled quickly to the edge and looked around.

He spotted the dark shape of the Pisaca, heading away down the ghat. She was holding the hand of a small child dressed in dark, baggy clothes. Pandu wondered who it was, as he hurried along the final section of the ledge and jumped down on to the ghat.

As the boy sped after the two figures, he didn't notice the turbaned priest leap up from his platform and pull a phone from the folds of his robe.

*

As soon as Lizzie opened the kitchen door Tubs leapt up at her and began licking her hands furiously. She dropped to her knees and held him around the sides.

'How did she know?' she hissed into his fur, her thoughts reeling. 'I never told her...'

She looked across at the window ledge, where her mobile had been discarded days ago. Her *useless* mobile. *But maybe it would have a signal now...*

Navigating the table and chairs by the moonlight coming in through the windows, Lizzie hurried over to it. She pushed the *on* button and waited for the screen to light up. Even if it worked, would her mum have her mobile with her? And turned on – *in a theatre?*

She cursed as the screen revealed a pathetic absence of reception bars. And then she checked herself.

Was she being hysterical?

She thought back carefully to the moment when Eva had come in. No, Lizzie was sure she'd only told her that her mum had gone out to see a play. *So how come she knew she was with Godwin?*

Lizzie told herself not to be paranoid. Eva and Godwin were friends. Perhaps he'd told her he was taking Lizzie's mum out.

But then why had Eva at first pretended not to know?

And – how had she got here tonight? There was no car in the drive. *Had she been spying on the house, waiting until her mum and Godwin had gone?*

Suddenly Lizzie heard a door bang in the hall, followed by the creak of floorboards. Mr Tubs began to growl. She grabbed him round the neck and pulled him back from the door, to the far side of the room.

After a few moments the kitchen door opened, and light from the lounge spilled in. Eva stepped down into the room, her front in shadow.

'What, no light?' said the woman, softly. 'Are you trying to save electricity?'

And then, despite her desperate attempt to pull him back, Mr Tubs broke free from Lizzie's grasp and launched himself towards the figure in the doorway…

*

When they reached the dark riverside edge of Manikarnika ghat, the woman and child stopped.

Pandu ducked behind a building as the Pisaca threw a glance over her shoulder. As he stood with his back against the wall, he drew out his mobile and fumbled a quick text message to Raj, which read simply:

Manikarnika

He had followed the Pisaca and child at a discreet distance along Dashashwamedha ghat and then to the temple of Lakshmi. As soon as the Pisaca spotted the police cordon surrounding the temple, she glanced around – Pandu briefly glimpsed her gaunt white face in the moonlight – and then hurried the child onwards, all the way to here. As he followed, Pandu wondered what he would do if she seemed about to harm the child, who he assumed from his gait was a boy. But luckily she made no threatening gestures, and the child seemed happy enough at her side. Perhaps he was a street kid, lured with a promise of food, or money? Again, Pandu wondered *where* they had come from.

When he looked back, he saw the woman and boy climbing over a low stone wall *into* the Manikarnika cremation ground. As soon as they were over, he dashed along the final section of riverbank and peered over the wall.

Beyond was a secluded section of the cremation ground, lit up by one lone fire, which was currently unattended. A temple wall separated the site from the main area of the burnings. At first, Pandu was sure the Pisaca and child had disappeared, but then, as he looked down towards the river edge, he spotted them, standing near a small stone structure.

Immediately, he realised what it was – another sacred well. He watched as the child pointed, and then the Pisaca got to her knees and reached down into the kund. She seemed to struggle for a moment, and then pulled something out from the hole. Pandu caught a glimpse of a large, egg-shaped stone, before she swaddled it in her cloak. Then they turned back towards the wall, and for the first time Pandu got a clear view of the child's face and his heart leapt with joy and terror.

It was Albi.

Without thinking, Pandu hoisted himself up, preparing to spring into the compound and rescue his brother from the killer. But, just as he straightened his arms, he felt someone grab his legs and yank him backwards.

He crashed down against the wall, and found himself face to face with a turbaned priest with bright eyes. He watched in horror as the priest produced a short handled dagger from his robes.

And then a voice behind the priest shouted: 'Freeze – Police!'

Hanu spun round to see Raj standing behind him, a gun in his good hand. Slowly, the cruel look on the priest's face subsided into one of resignation. He raised his hands.

'Drop the knife!' shouted Raj, moving forward.

'OK,' said the priest. He appeared about to let go of the blade, but suddenly his arm swung swiftly back, preparing to hurl it at the Inspector.

A gunshot rang out, and Hanu fell on his back. Pandu watched in horror as blood blossomed on the priest's white robe. Then he looked at Raj, whose expression was grim.

'Albi's in the cremation ground with the Pisaca!' said Pandu.

Raj ran up beside him and they both looked over the wall.

'My God,' said Raj. 'Not *them* again...'

In the cremation area, Albi and the cloaked woman were now being surrounded by the three black-skinned creatures, goaded on by the Kali priestess, Lamya. The cloaked woman was clutching something to her chest, as the feral creatures moved in, hissing and spitting.

Tears filled Pandu's eyes. 'What are we going to...' he said, but stopped, seeing Raj speaking into his phone.

'Yes – move in now!' said the Inspector urgently. 'It's the women, and the priestess – *and* the Pisaca! They're all here! Move, move!'

In the next moment, Pandu saw the huge figure of Sergeant Singh and half-a-dozen policemen appear from around the corner of the temple wall. They were all carrying revolvers.

Wincing with pain, Raj swung himself over the wall and yelled:

'Everyone stay where you are! You're all under arrest!'

Then everything went wild.

With a couple of quick, barked commands from Lamya, two of the Daginis charged Singh's police officers, whilst the third sprinted at Ashlyn. Still clutching the lump of stone, Ashlyn grabbed Albi's hand and tried to run back towards the river, but the Dagini was fast and soon caught her up and wrenched her back by the cloak.

Meanwhile, Singh lost no time in commanding his men to open fire. One young man with a moustache hesitated – evidently unsure about shooting an unarmed woman – and in the next moment he was on his back with his face in the creature's rabid mouth. The sight of one of their colleagues going down was enough to bolster the remaining officers, who began shooting at the other woman. Singh ran forward with another policeman and together they wrenched the first Dagini off the prostrate man's body. With a mighty bellow, Singh hurled her into the funeral pyre.

Landing in the middle of the flames, the Dagini screamed – a long, agonising caterwaul – and then, to the amazement of Singh and his fellow officer, she seemed to collapse into dust.

'Get them into the fire!' shouted Singh, and the men rushed the nearby Dagini, pistols blazing.

Meanwhile Raj and Pandu were running towards Ashlyn, who had been brought down by the third Dagini. The stone egg, rolling down the mud towards the river, was stopped by Albi's foot. The boy bent down and picked it up, but as soon as he looked up Lamya was standing over him.

'Give it to me,' she said.

'No!' he shouted, swinging it away from her outstretched hands. But as he tried to run she grabbed the hood of his baggy sweatshirt and yanked him back towards her, seizing the stone. Albi screamed.

And then Lamya was knocked clear sideways by Pandu running at full pace. The boy came down on top of her heavily, and the stone went flying from her grasp.

'Don't touch my brother!' he shouted, and with one solid blow from his fist knocked her out.

Raj heard a scream and ran towards the third Dagini, who was grappling with Ashlyn. The creature had pinned the witch down, and was pushing her jaw upwards with its elbow. It looked as if at any moment Ashlyn's head might break off her neck.

Realising that he might actually be *rescuing* the Pisaca, the Inspector ran up alongside the Dagini and shot her in the side of the head. Ashlyn spun over on the dirt coughing terribly whilst the Inspector grabbed the gibbering black-skinned woman whose face was now half missing, and dragged her slowly towards the fire.

'Get *her* – it's the Pisaca!' he shouted to Singh, indicating the choking figure of Ashlyn. Then, with

271

grim determination, the Inspector dragged the Dagini the final few paces to the fire and shoved her in. He turned away and marched back towards Ashlyn, not watching as the creature exploded in the flames.

Pandu clutched Albi, tears rolling down his cheeks. 'You're safe now, little brother,' he said. 'Safe from the Pisaca...'

Feeling his brother's arms around him, Albi was overcome by emotion and for a few moments all he could do was utter a series of inarticulate sobs.

'You're safe from her now, safe,' repeated Pandu.

Albi finally found the words he was looking for. 'Have... have you caught her, then?'

Pandu looked round to where Raj and Singh were standing over the figure of Ashlyn, who was coughing and spitting in the dust.

'Yes,' he said. 'That's her.'

Albi looked round. 'No it's not,' he said.

Chapter 19: A Transformation

'What the…' began Eva, as the little dog launched himself up at her.

'Tubs!' Lizzie shouted, but the dog ignored her, and in the next moment he was tearing at Eva's sleeve.

'Get off!' cried Eva, tugging her arm free from the dog's jaws. But Tubs leapt at her again, and sank his teeth into her leg.

'Get… off!'

Tubs refused to let go. Eva shook her leg, banging into the kitchen table, but the dog only redoubled his efforts, snarling and growling.

'Tubs – *let her go*!' Lizzie shrieked. Even in the dim light, she could see how distorted Eva's face was becoming with pain and rage.

And then, as Tubs continued to savage the tall woman's calf, something strange happened. The air in the kitchen seemed to become colder, and drier, and suddenly everything was sharper, more crystal clear, as if the light from the moon was increasing. Eva gave out a huge and astounding roar – more like a weightlifter than a woman – and kicked the dog across the room. At the same moment Lizzie staggered back horrified as the woman's face seemed to change out of all proportion, becoming increasingly ridged and swollen. Eva's jaw came forward and stretched and then, as she bellowed again, fangs began to sprout like twigs in her mouth.

And, in that moment, Lizzie realised the terrible truth – *Eva was the Pisaca!*

As Eva's features continued to transform, Lizzie looked on with a strangely detached mixture of horror and fascination. Her mind whirled, as things fell into place. Everything she'd suspected – since encountering the black-skinned women and reading her great-uncle's thoughts on mythical beings – was true. There *were* supernatural creatures, and the Pisaca – *Eva* – was one of them. And, as Lizzie watched the skin of the woman whom she'd so trusted warp, crack, and blister, she wondered if Eva might be one of the most powerful demons of all. Her eyes dropped to the creature's hands, where long talons were now splitting their fingertips. She frowned, noticing how the bandage was coming loose and exposing nasty black welts.

That was no horse bite... she thought fleetingly, before she realised that the transformation was complete and the Pisaca was standing tall and foreboding above her. Another rush of fear paralyzed her. She wanted to scream, but her voice stuck in her throat.

'You stupid child,' growled the Pisaca, stepping towards her. 'Now – tell me everything you know about the Lingam!'

'*Eva…*' Lizzie whispered pleadingly, tears stinging her eyes.

And then there was another, more animal, growl, and once again Mr Tubs was snapping at the creature's heels.

Eva screeched and tried to stamp on Tubs, but the small dog leapt lithely aside and then sprang and caught her injured hand in its jaws. Eva cried out, and shook her arm furiously. Tubs managed to hold on for a few moments, his paws flailing about in the air, but then lost his grip and flew back into the corner of the room. Lizzie watched in horror as he collapsed motionless on his side.

Then her instincts took over. Without pausing to think, she thrust herself between the cursing Pisaca and the door, and ran through into the lounge. Barely noticing as she bashed against the sofa, she was soon out in the hall and then into the study. Within moments she'd hurled open the glass door and was running past the sun dial towards the gap in the hedge. Risking a quick glance behind, she saw the giant figure of the Pisaca coming through the warmly lit study after her.

'*God!*' she cried, and fled down the dark, yew-scented corridor towards the Indian garden...

*

As Lizzie came to in the underground alcove, she knew things were different.

Two lamps were suspended from the ceiling of the chamber, vividly revealing the gunge on the walls and the yellowed bones and skulls sticking out from the dark water. A young, clean-shaven policeman was standing on a ledge near the doorway.

As she dropped down on to the floor, the policeman exclaimed something in Hindi.

'Look – get your gun out – the Pisaca is behind me!' she screamed, running towards him.

'What?' he said.

'The Pisaca! She's following me! She's going to come out of that alcove any moment...'

'How did you get in here?'

'Don't worry about that! The Pisaca...' Lizzie froze, as Eva's dark head began to appear against the stone.

'What on earth...?' said the policeman.

Desperately, Lizzie leapt at him and tried to undo the catch of his holster. Instinctively the man pulled away from her.

'Get off!' he shouted, seizing her arm and beginning to undo the gun himself.

But as soon as she looked round Lizzie realised it was too late – Eva was through, dropping heavily from the alcove on to the chamber floor.

'Run!' Lizzie screamed at the man and, as he let go of her arm in surprise, she began to dash for the door.

The policeman tugged his revolver out and pointed it at the Pisaca as she rushed towards him.

'Stop!' he screamed, and fired straight into her.

The bullet ploughed into Eva's chest, making her stagger back a couple of steps, but in the next moment she rushed forward at the man. Lizzie caught a glimpse of sharp talons closing around the man's neck, and then she turned and rushed up the steps, trying to ignore the terrible screams behind her.

She came out on to the ledge and looked through tear-blurred eyes at the glittering moonlit water of the Ganges. Trying to shut out the rabid snarls and shouts still coming from the chamber below, she shuffled quickly round and jumped down on to the ghat.

Then she heard a shout of something she couldn't make out, and turned to see another policeman in the shadow of the temple wall.

'Help! Help – it's the *Pisaca!*' she yelled.

'What?' said the man.

'The Pisaca's down there – she's attacking the other man!'

The bearded man pressed the button of the radio strapped to his uniform. He began to speak in Hindi: 'Hello Inspector – yes, we need backup, fast. I have a witness reporting that the Pisaca is at the old temple... a girl, yes...what?...You're nearby?... Yes, I'll...'

Lizzie glanced back at the temple and froze as the Pisaca appeared at the corner on the ledge. Despite her talons and her size, the monster was moving with incredible speed and agility, like a giant spider.

'Stop her!' she screeched, as the policeman stopped talking and gaped.

'Shoot her!'

The man pulled his gun from the holster and fired at the cloaked form. The Pisaca cried out, but kept coming.

'Shoot her again – she's not... *normal!*' shouted Lizzie.

The man fired four more shots into the creature. The Pisaca shook with each bullet, but continued to shuffle around. Just as she was twisting to leap on to the ghat, the man fired his last shot, which made her lose her footing. Lizzie watched as the demon fell down and splashed into the river.

'What *was* she?' said the man, turning to Lizzie.

For a moment Lizzie didn't reply. Then she whispered: 'What *is* she...' and the policeman followed her gaze down to the water where a black arm was breaking free from the surface.

'She's not going to die!' shouted Lizzie. 'Run!'

The policeman didn't need any more convincing, and they began to sprint down the deserted ghat.

As they ran, Lizzie glanced back over her shoulder and saw that the Pisaca was out of the water and speeding after them. *She would catch them any moment.* Lizzie looked at the ghats and buildings ahead of them, to see if there was anyone else around, or anywhere else they could try to get to – perhaps a boat they could jump into? But, in the darkness, there was no-one else around, and no other possibilities of escape.

'She's right behind us,' shouted the policeman as they ran.

'I know,' cried Lizzie.

'You keep running,' he said.

'What...'

And suddenly the bearded man stopped, and turned.

'Halt! You're under arrest!' he shouted, holding up his pistol at the looming demon.

'No!' shouted Lizzie, stopping too and looking around. She knew what he was doing was futile.

He threw her another quick look and shouted determinedly: 'Run!' And then he crashed down on to the ghat as the Pisaca collided with him.

For a moment Lizzie watched in horror as the policeman thrashed wildly about, struggling to keep the fearsome creature's jaws away from his throat. And then she yelled:

'Get off him, Eva!'

Pinning the man down with her clawed hands, the Pisaca looked up. Lizzie winced at the sight of her cruelly misshapen features.

'Come here, Lizzie,' croaked the demon, in a thick, guttural voice.

'If I come, you'll let him go?'

'Yes.'

Suddenly, out of the corner of her eye, Lizzie noticed four shadowy figures coming down the ghats towards them. They were behind Eva, so she couldn't see them. Perhaps the man had called for backup, she hoped fleetingly. *But, even if he had, what could they do?*

Despite every instinct telling her to run, she began to walk towards the crouched Pisaca. As she did so, she noticed that the shadowy figures were now running towards them.

'Don't hurt him,' she said, as she came up in front of the demon. She saw that the policeman's face was pressed sideways down against the stone ghat by the Pisaca's hand. His eyes were closed, and Lizzie prayed he was just unconscious.

Slowly, the Pisaca stood up. And, at that moment, there came another cry:

'Stop!'

Lizzie and Eva looked round to see the leader of the approaching group. Suddenly Lizzie realised who it was – Raj, with Pandu behind him, and a small boy, and – *no, it couldn't be* – Ashlyn! Pandu was running awkwardly, clutching something against his side, and Raj's arm was bandaged in a sling.

Lizzie's relief evaporated almost immediately. How could they stop the Pisaca? *Perhaps a whole group of policemen, armed with machine guns, could have done something...*

'Get back – she's invulnerable!' she yelled.

But the boys, policeman, and witch kept coming. Lizzie turned and screamed as she saw the Pisaca was now lunging towards her with her taloned hands outstretched. She tried to dive out of the way but Eva caught hold of her top and yanked her back. In the next moment she was pinned against the demon, and a thick nail was pressing against her throat.

'Stay where you are or I'll kill her!' the Pisaca growled – and the group stopped, a few feet away from

Eva and Lizzie at the water's edge. Raj scowled, unable to train his gun on the demon because of Lizzie, and Pandu cursed in anguish. Albi cowered behind his brother, shaking with fear.

'I knew it was you!' shouted Ashlyn. Despite the grotesque distortion of the lower face and jaw, the forehead and eyes were still recognisably Eva's.

'Well done, you,' said the Pisaca. Suddenly she spotted Pandu, and the object he was clutching at his side. 'What's that?' she said.

'This?' said Pandu, holding the Lingam up in both hands. 'It's what you want, isn't it?'

Eva's eyes blazed. 'Take off your shirt, wrap the Lingam in it and pass it to me,' she hissed.

'Maybe I'll just chuck it in the river,' said Pandu insolently.

Eva squeezed Lizzie, and pressed a talon hard against her jugular. Struggling for breath, Lizzie smelt the odious, rusty smell she'd noticed all those nights ago in the Indian garden. *The smell Eva had covered with her perfume – the smell of blood.*

'Do as I say, or I'll find it in the river myself – after I've ripped your throats out!'

With a glance at Raj and Ashlyn, Pandu reluctantly set the stone down and pulled his shirt off over his head. He then wrapped the Lingam up and held it out towards the Pisaca. Lizzie felt the creature's breath quicken.

'Good,' she said. 'Bring it closer – *closer*...'

Pandu took a couple of slow steps down towards them. He threw Lizzie a quick glance.

'Now – put it down.'

Slowly, Pandu bent down, not taking his eyes off the Pisaca. He placed the Lingam carefully on the stone step, and then straightened up. The Pisaca's head strained forward in excitement, and Lizzie felt the nail pushing tighter against her throat. She struggled to ease the pressure, worried that the creature was so intent on the Lingam she might kill her by accident.

Then, as Pandu began to step away, he suddenly swung his foot up and kicked the Lingam as if it were a football. He let out a yelp of pain and clutched his foot as the egg-shaped stone bounced quickly down the steps towards the river.

'No!' screamed the Pisaca. Without thinking, she released Lizzie and leapt sideways to stop the stone. At the same moment Raj fired his revolver, and the bullet struck the monster in the hand as she was reaching out towards the Lingam. As Eva shouted with pain and anger, Lizzie realised she had the chance to grab the stone before her. Without even noticing that the Inspector was preparing to fire again, she leapt across and stooped to snatch up the Lingam, at the same time barging the Pisaca with her shoulder.

Ashlyn realised Raj was just about to shoot and jumped into the Inspector's outstretched firing arm, knocking the pistol upwards. The bullet whistled narrowly over Lizzie's head, as she pulled the Lingam out of the unravelled shirt and spun back to face Eva. The demon was about to grab her but, seeing the unwrapped Lingam, she froze.

As Lizzie stared up into those deep, brown eyes – *Eva's eyes* – she thought, even in the moonlight, she saw a mixture of emotion – fear, greed, loathing, *hope*…

'Lizzie, give it to me… I… I *need* it. I can give you anything you want. You're special, you can have it all, with my help,' said Eva.

'Eva?' said Lizzie, feeling tears well in her eyes. 'Why…?'

'It's hard to explain… my kind – which is not so different from *your* kind – is being… *drawn*… away to another place, somewhere dark and unknown. Somewhere from which we may never return – but with the power of the Lingam and the tirthas and… a few other artefacts… I can stop it happening. And I can help *you* to live longer – much longer – and gain special powers too…'

As Eva spoke, Lizzie noticed she was coming closer, at the same time slowly binding her hand in the shredded bandage which still hung from it.

'Please, Lizzie.' The rough voice struggled to sustain a softened tone. 'Give it to me.'

Lizzie shook her head slowly. 'You *killed* all those children.'

'It's… how I have to live – but the Lingam can change all that.'

Lizzie's eyebrows lifted as she stared into Eva's eyes, now tender and kind, as she remembered them from the party and the ride…

'No,' she said, taking a step back. 'You can't have it!'

And then the anger reappeared on the distorted face, and suddenly Eva – *the Pisaca* – was lunging forward again, snatching at the Lingam with her swaddled hand.

But instead of running Lizzie used all her strength to hurl the stone up into Eva's face. For a moment Lizzie saw the bewilderment in the demon's eyes, and then the Lingam smashed into them.

There was a dull roar – whether from the Pisaca or elsewhere it was impossible to tell – and then a shower of silver-black threads and sparks whipped up and around the demon. Lizzie stepped back in horror as the strange, electrical activity intensified into a cone shape rising up from the creature. Eva seemed to fall backwards and then the static whirlwind increased and for the first time Lizzie felt as if she was watching the tirtha plane *from the outside*. Surreal things – fluttering, membranous wings, a body with a hippo's head, a babyish face with ugly fangs – seemed to swirl up and down the cone, surrounded by a broiling mass of black-white stars.

Then there was a terrible, disembodied scream and Lizzie was sure she saw the writhing creature rise up suddenly, helplessly, through the maelstrom at the centre of the cone. In the next moment, the demon vanished amid the chaotic, pulsing vacuum – and everything stopped.

In the hush that followed Lizzie stood numbly, staring at the simple shape of the Lingam which was resting on the lowest ghat. The policeman who'd so bravely defended her was beginning to cough, as Raj knelt over him. But of Eva there remained no trace, not even the blood-stained bandage.

Lizzie felt Pandu's arm around her shoulder.

'It's OK,' he said. 'It's all OK.'

Lizzie's eyes filled with tears. 'I have to go back,' she said, her mind reeling. 'I think my dog's hurt…'

*

As they came back down into the underground chamber, Raj ran to the man who had been attacked by the Pisaca.

'Is he all right?' asked Ashlyn.

'I can't feel a pulse,' said Raj. 'Look – you lot take Lizzie back through that… *portal*, or whatever it is. I'll wait for the ambulance and take care of the other man – and the Lingam.'

Ashlyn went first through the tirtha, to show Pandu what to do.

'By Brahma, Vishnu, and Shiva, I thought I'd seen everything…' said the boy, as he watched the witch disappear. 'Are you sure this is safe?'

Lizzie nodded. 'Trust me,' she said.

Then, shaking his head, the teenage boy pushed himself headfirst into the deep-set alcove. Albi, nodding briefly at Lizzie, went through next.

Before she jumped up, Lizzie paused and turned to Raj, who was still kneeling by the prostrate man.

'Goodbye, Inspector,' she said.

'Thank you, Lizzie,' he said softly, and she could see that there were tears in his eyes.

Then she turned back, and followed Albi through the tirtha.

As soon as she came round on the snowy lawn she felt something warm and familiar lapping against her cheek. Opening her eyes she saw Mr Tubs standing there, shivering excitedly in the cold. Ashlyn, Albi and Pandu were standing beside her smiling – and there was another dog-like creature beside the witch, which Lizzie quickly realised was a fox.

'You're all right!' she exclaimed to Tubs, and clutched him close against her. The small dog barked, and rubbed his side against her. 'Thank God,' she said, and burst into tears.

Chapter 20: Reconciliation

'So – you found out about the tirtha and this priest-friend of Great-Uncle Eric's – *Bakir* – through reading the diaries?' Despite being wrapped in a blanket by the fire in the study, Lizzie could still feel her hands and legs shaking. She couldn't believe Eva – *the Pisaca* – had been sitting in this chair only a short while ago. *She couldn't believe it.*

'Yes,' said Ashlyn, who was sitting opposite her at her great-uncle's desk. 'The study window had been left ajar, so I climbed in and took them, soon after Eric died. I was suspicious because he'd told me about the intruder in the garden. It didn't take me long – after I recovered from the shock of the tirtha – to *suspect* the intruder was the Pisaca, using the tirtha to kill – and to evade capture.'

'When did you realise Albi was the wild boy?' asked Lizzie. She looked across at the small boy, sitting on a chair sipping his steaming hot chocolate. Beside him, Pandu sat cross-legged on the tiled hearth. Both boys were also swaddled in blankets.

'I realised it was probably him after my first meeting with Bakir. Bakir thought the Pisaca might have captured Albi and brought him through to find out where this Lingam was. We agreed he would continue to search for Albi in Kashi, whilst I – with the help of Lugh, my familiar – tried to establish some trust with the 'wild boy' here, and find out if it was Albi.'

'What's a familiar?' said Pandu. As he spoke he glanced around the room, still trying to adjust to the strange miracle of his surroundings.

'It's an animal which forms a special bond with a Wiccan,' said Ashlyn. 'I know it sounds strange. But it's perfectly natural for us. Lugh is a fox, and he helped save Albi from the hunters – as well as doing a few other things.'

Lizzie recalled seeing the fox darting away in the Indian garden, and out the back of Limetree Cottage. Under normal circumstances, she'd have been astonished by what Ashlyn was saying, but after the Pisaca she still felt numb, as if nothing could ever surprise her again. *Would she ever get over what had happened?*

'It's lucky you still had the Lingam with you when the guard radioed Raj,' she said.

'We were on the way to the Blue Temple, to hand it back to the priests,' said Pandu.

'But... *what* were they?' said Lizzie. 'I mean, the Pisaca, and those women-things? Were they really creatures from this tirtha *plane*?'

'I'm not sure we'll ever know,' said Ashlyn, pensively.

They sat in silence, thinking about the scale of the mystery, and the huge changes it meant to their lives. Lizzie thought about the Lingam, and what Eva had said to her in her final moments, about helping Lizzie to obtain special powers. She felt giddy, and tears welled in her eyes as she again recalled the horror of Eva's transformation.

'Come here,' said Ashlyn, reaching out and putting her arm around her. 'You'll be all right, Lizzie.' She looked at Pandu and Albi. 'You've all been through so much. You've seen more strange things and dealt with more – *much* more – than most people ever will. But remember, I'm always here for you. And remember how special you are. You've defeated a terrible woman – a *demon* – and helped save the children of Kashi. You're all remarkable.'

Lizzie found it strange to be hugging the woman who only a few hours ago she'd thought was a killer. But, as she pressed herself into the warm folds of the woman's cloak, she felt a sudden, peculiar sense of kinship.

'Even though he only saw you once, at your christening, your great-uncle always said you were special,' Ashlyn whispered.

Despite her sadness, Lizzie felt a flicker of pride. 'But I… I trusted Eva so much,' she said. She couldn't believe how deceitful she'd been. *It was such a betrayal.* Pandu reached up and held her hand.

'Are you going to speak to your mum about this?' asked Ashlyn.

Lizzie looked up at the clock, and saw that it was nearly eleven. *It was incredible, everything had happened in the course of one ordinary evening.* She took a deep breath. *Not* telling her mum felt impossible – but so did telling her. All she wanted to do was cry.

'No – I'm going to try not to.' Instinctively, she knew that keeping it to herself – *and her new companions* – was the right thing to do. But she couldn't even begin to say why.

'If you need me, you know where I am,' said Ashlyn.

'And you know where we are, too,' said Pandu, smiling.

Lizzie looked at him fondly. 'Yes, thanks,' she said.

As Ashlyn, Pandu and Albi headed out into the garden Lizzie noticed the fox again, sniffing around the base of the sundial. As soon as it saw them it came up and brushed against Ashlyn's legs.

'I owe you a lot, Mr Lugh,' said Pandu, bowing elaborately to the creature and reminding Lizzie of one of Dick Pike's theatrical gestures. She wondered what the real bond was between Ashlyn and her *familiar*. And then, curiously, she thought of Mr Tubs, who was standing proudly at her side, watching the others go.

'Come and see me soon, in the cottage,' said Ashlyn. 'We've got a lot to talk about.'

'Will you tell me about Eric?' said Lizzie.

'Yes,' said Ashlyn. A momentary sadness crossed her face. 'I will. I'll tell you all about him.'

When they'd gone, Lizzie felt a crushing tiredness, worse even than the fatigue she'd felt upon her first return from Kashi. Putting the guard in front of the fire, and then nudging Tubs into his basket, she was soon upstairs and in bed.

As soon as she turned the light out she was asleep. She didn't even hear her mum being dropped back by Godwin.

*

The next morning Lizzie woke late, to a mass of aches and pains. All her muscles were stiff, she had scratches on her hands and legs, and her neck was bruised. As her mind began to churn with panic, she leapt out of bed and threw on her clothes. She *had* to talk to her mum about last night, no matter how absurd it sounded...

But as she came downstairs and heard her mum singing in the lounge she stopped.

What could she say? *Surely it was better to go back and talk to Ashlyn, who understood everything?*

Mr Tubs was the first to greet her as she came into the living room, wagging his stumpy tail. He watched her uncertainly, as if trying to sense how well she was. She reached out and touched his nose.

As soon as Lizzie's mum looked up from dusting she exclaimed:

'Lizzie – look at your hair! You look as if you've been sleeping rough! You could have brushed it before you came down.'

They stood and looked at each other in silence. For the first time, Lizzie noticed the wrinkles around her mum's eyes, and it crossed her mind that her mum was getting older.

'Mum...' she began, and tears filled her eyes.

'What is it?' said her mum, coming forward and hugging her. As soon as she was in her mum's embrace, Lizzie began to cry uncontrollably.

'It's not Godwin, is it? Honestly, we're only friends.'

'No,' Lizzie said. She sobbed, then added: 'But… be careful about him, Mum. Please.'

'He's all right – he's a real gentleman.'

'Mum!'

'Yes, I will, of course.'

Lizzie continued to cry.

'Lizzie…' Her mum kissed her hair.

'You were right…to be suspicious… about Eva,' Lizzie whispered.

'What's that?'

'Nothing.'

Finally, in the warmth of her mum's arms, Lizzie's tears stopped.

'Do you want us to go back to London?' said her mum.

For a moment Lizzie was quiet. Then she said:

'No.'

Epilogue: New Year

Five weeks later, on the morning of New Year's Day, Lizzie woke up with one word in her head: *tirthas.*

Tirthas. *Plural.* Whenever they were mentioned in her great-uncle's diaries, it was always in the plural. And when Eva was speaking to her, she'd referred to them in the plural. Briefly Lizzie shuddered, thinking how everyone in the village now thought Eva had returned to one of her foreign homes.

Were there more tirthas, hidden in the other rooms?

After breakfast, she went out with Tubs through a miserable drizzle into the room with the three primitive-looking wooden heads. The *Easter Island* garden.

Cautiously, she peered at the largest head, which nearly came up to her shoulders. The rain had soaked into the grooves, darkening its slanted, empty eyes and highlighting its nostrils and lips. She noticed how it was sunk into the soil of the overgrown, grassy border.

One by one, she pushed the statues to see if they would move.

The largest was too heavy, the middle-sized one shifted slightly, but the smallest she had to quickly stop from tipping over into the hedge. Nothing else happened. She knelt down and began to prod eyes, noses, ears, and lips. She pushed down hard on the crowns to see if they would go down further into the ground. She tried to twist the faces round.

Then she sat down on the little one and cursed.

After a while she had another idea, and stepped up on to the lowest head. She made a small jump, then stepped up on to the middle one and jumped again. Nothing happened. Without hope, she stepped up from that on to the largest one and made another little jump, just to complete the sequence.

Nothing happened. She glanced at Tubs.

'Not helping me today then, pooch?' she said. He gave her one of his more enigmatic, quizzical looks.

Then, because it was a little too high to jump off the big one, she stepped back down on to the middle one and then on to the small one and then, just as her foot was about to hit the ground, the garden began to fizz and blur and change into riotous colours...

*

After an unknown period, she came round in a rocky, shaded space, blinking away images of solemn faces and dazzling, reflected light.

She was right, she thought dreamily, lying on her back. There *were* more.

And then panic seized her and she sprang up, looking quickly around. But, aside from a few pale markings on the rock which gave an impression of eyes and wings, there was nothing else in the cave. Her nerves settled. The next thing she did was push herself back hard into the crevice, to check the process reversed safely enough.

Finding that it did, she returned to the cave, and slowly crept out into the light.

She emerged on to a windswept beach, looking out across a choppy, green-grey sea. At either end of the beach, jagged bluffs rose from crashing waves. The air was cold and fresh, laced with briny spray.

Lizzie turned and looked back at the small cave, and the island beyond. Rough grassy slopes rose gently upwards, punctuated by dark stone statues – strange, thoughtful heads, similar to those in the garden, but many times larger. The giant heads – all ten or twelve of them – faced up towards the centre of the island, as if waiting for something.

Briefly, she thought back to her first transportation to Kashi, and how scared and bewildered she'd been in that dark chamber – and all that had happened since. *What would her dad have made of it?*

He would have been so proud of her. That she was having adventures – *incredible adventures* – on her own. She smiled, and looked back at the giant heads.

Then, as she watched, a great white bird appeared, its long wings bent on the currents of the air, its gaze focused on the distant, hazy horizon. The bird flew high over the centre of the island, above the curved line of statues, and right over Lizzie's upturned face, before heading out across the wild sea.

Pulling up her hood, Lizzie whooped with joy as she watched the white bird go.

If you enjoyed this book, please leave a review at your favourite online retailer.

An Excerpt from

Book 2 of The Secret of the Tirthas:

The Book of Life

Chapter 1: Plat Eyes

In the deep water there is pain and loss and endless, dispiriting grey, and then there are flames and snakes in skulls. There is the draw and pull and greed for the fire of life, the hunger that spans across time, the hunger for that which those who are living have now but do not comprehend and will lose, a hunger borne by those long gone, who sit in the swirling silts at the bottom of the water, soaked through to the core with cold and lifeless wet.

Theirs is a constant, fidgety greed.

*

They – whatever *they* were – were coming for her now, through the darkening swamp.

300

As she ran, bounding from one clump of bog grass to the next, weaving in and out of blackened tree stumps, desperately trying to avoid bubbling pools of greenish mud, Lizzie heard their mournful groans, interspersed with guttural snarls. *What were they?*

And *why oh why* had she been mad enough to go through another tirtha?

'You idiot!' she muttered to herself as she leapt into a mass of exposed tree root and had to scrabble about with her hands and feet to keep propelling herself forward. The stink from the marsh in front of her face was disgusting, all egg and wet and earth and toilets.

She realised she was losing any hope of finding her way back to the tirtha again – and had to force that idea straight out of her head. *One thing at a time.*

Glancing over her shoulder she saw the dark outline of one of *them* taking shape amidst the misty trees. From a distance he looked like a stumbling drunk, but after she'd transported from Miss Day's garden and come out of that reeking pool she'd seen him close up, and the eyes had assured her this was no ordinary man.

A groan came from her left and she turned to catch sight of another, smaller figure, wading towards her through a tract of smoking swamp.

Screaming, she leapt free from the tree roots and splashed wildly through a section of clear but thankfully shallow water. Through the dense latticework of branches she glimpsed another pale light like one she'd spotted earlier, but as soon as she began to hope it might be a house or car it vanished again.

'Help!' she shouted. Her heart bludgeoned itself against her ribcage.

Another of the creatures bellowed from a short distance behind her. She looked back in terror, catching a glimpse of the twilight moon high above the trees and then seeing the haggard, slime-coated face of a man leering at her through the fog. And then, as she looked back to check where she was running she screamed again because there, standing right in front of her, was a young girl.

Lizzie skidded and slipped, and ended up on one knee in the water, staring up in disbelief at the figure.

The girl had a mass of very blonde, almost-white hair, and was wearing an old-fashioned dress embroidered with pearly beads. Her pale skin and rosebud lips were fuzzy, as if she were standing behind a muslin curtain. In fact her whole body was insubstantial, shimmering with soft light in the darkness. Her eyes alone seemed fully present, sharp and intense, dark brown verging on black.

That way.

The girl's mouth had moved, but Lizzie was sure no sound had come from it. *But she'd heard the words in her head.*

She looked in the direction of the girl's pointing finger into a gloomy mass of waterlogged forest.

'Wha...' she began, but the girl was gone.

Lizzie felt a cold hand on her shoulder.

She yelped and tugged herself down and away from the man behind her. He hadn't got a proper hold and she came free and once more she was running – running, running, *running* for her life, in the direction she'd been told to go. *By a ghost girl.*

Also Available Now

The Dreamer Falls – *Book 3 of The Secret of the Tirthas*

ABOUT THE AUTHOR

Steve Griffin grew up in Warwickshire and has worked for youth and environmental organisations in Wales and London. He has had poems published in Poetry Ireland, The New Welsh Review, and The Rialto.

The Secret of the Tirthas was inspired by trips to India, Africa, and the US, as well as a real 'garden of rooms' deep in the English countryside.

He now lives in the Surrey Hills with his wife and two young sons.

If you want to be the first to hear about new books, you can subscribe to his mailing list at: stevegriffin40@outlook.com

To find out more and see photos of the garden and other settings that inspired *The Secret of the Tirthas*, check out steve-griffin.com.

You can buy *The Secret of the Tirthas* in ebook format at most major online retailers, and in paperback at Amazon.

Made in the USA
Columbia, SC
02 July 2017